Sex & Attention II

SahKe Productions

Atlanta, GA 30339

http://www.sahkeproductions.com

sahkeproductions@gmail.com

Ordering Information:
Quantity sales. Special discounts are available on quantity
purchases by corporations, associations, and others. For details,
contact the publisher at the website or email above.

Printed in the United States of America

Sex & Attention II
Series: Sex & Attention

ISBN-13:
978-0692828410 (SahKe Productions)

Dedication

This book is dedicated to all my wonderful readers across the world who make me want to keep writing. I love you and thank you.

Books by Sasha Owens

Voices Unveiled

Sex & Attention

Sex & Attention II

Sex & Attention II

Contents

Prologue

How did I let one heartbreak allow me to drift this far? How did I get tangled in this love affair with two best friends who were practically brothers? I tried to fight it with everything inside of me, but Kich was an animal. He preyed on me every time I tried to leave. But I can't solely blame him. Kich showed me a side of me that I tried to hide for ages. I wanted to believe that it was just a phase that I would outgrow eventually. I buried it for a long time. I never knew why I was so attracted to cuffs, whippings, being choked during sex, degradation, etc. I wasn't mistreated as a child, so that can kill the misinterpretation that BDSM love comes from a trauma filled past because it doesn't. I was surrounded by love my entire life and I still was. I had parents who loved me, best friends who adored me, and tons of followers on social media lol. I was such a submissive at heart and BDSM was the most erotic way to indulge in that part of me. BDSM allowed me to be bound and free at the same time. I didn't have to pretend. I could touch the marks on my legs that were left from the rope that Daddy had bound me in. I didn't have to be ashamed to admit that I wanted my nipples clamped and yanked on. To the world I was weird, but to BDSM I was normal. I fit in there. This was me. Kich had truly set me free and I couldn't thank him enough. However, it seems just when I thought life was simple I was thrown another twist. How long do you think a woman will allow sex and attention to replace her one true desire...love?

Chapter 1
<u>Exposed</u>

"You're a fucking moron," I said.

Kich grabbed my neck and threw my head back into the car. I could feel the cold metal against my naked body.

"You love it," he said as he bit my bottom lip.

The difference in Kich's bites were that he didn't let go once it started to hurt. He bit me sometimes until I drew blood.

"What are we vampires?" I asked.

"We can be whatever you want to be Vistoria. There are no limits with me," he said.

"I like that," I replied as I looked into his eyes.

Kich was bad. He was horrible for me. I never knew what to expect, but he was perfect. Kich was honest. He didn't hide anything about him like Zay. With Zay I never knew what I was getting. I never knew if Zay truly loved me or if Zay was lonely and enjoyed the sex.

Fuck... Zay.

I had totally forgot he was in the house sleep after our makeup sex had knocked him out.

"You have to go before Zay wakes up," I said.

"What?" Kich asked surprised.

"No, I'm about to go in and speak," he said.

"Kich, stop being an asshole. That's not even funny," I said.

"Who's playing," he said and pulled his pants up.

I threw my big T-shirt back on and jumped in front of him.

"Kich don't do this," I begged.

"Why are you still hiding Vistoria?" he asked.

"Kich I'm not ready to tell him," I continued.

He kept walking towards the door.

I stopped and looked at the ground.

"Please," I murmured.

I then felt his presence closer to me and then he snatched my body into his.

"You really love him. You're willing to protect him even after the way he has hurt you?" Kich gritted his teeth.

"It's not that easy Kich. No one understands but his heart means well," I said.

"Does his heart mean well or does his heart just know self-gain?" he asked.

"What does that mean?" I asked irritated.

"Is it possible to love selfishly?" Kich asked.

Conditionally

Do you love me?
Like really love me?
I find myself asking these questions.
It appears you're always by my side, so helpful.
But is it possible to love selfishly?

See as time goes, your love seems to be conditioned.
You love me enough to get me to please you but in an instance, you've changed.
We don't go out anymore, you never invite me to your events, there's someone new, but you still say you love me.

You love us in different ways and you say I'll always have a place.
We've been in this for over a decade but I just figured out the cycle.
I use to laugh and joke about how you did other people...
straddling them along until they served their purpose in your life.
You'd then cut them off, cold.
The emotions had gotten old, you no longer could use them.
I saw you repeat this cycle over and over.
I even knew when the chopping block was coming.
I never knew I was on this block, I thought you loved me differently.
This caricature I had of you wouldn't hurt me, this
is just funny.
But your character is where I just shouldn't have bet money.
This is you.
You're this way to everyone, how could I be so dumb.....to think I was different.

"Think on that for a while," he kissed me on my nose and walked back towards his car.

"Kich," I turned around.

"Yes Vistoria," he said.

"I don't want you to go," I said.

"Vistoria you know we both can't stay," Kich said.

"I know," and then I hugged him.

I loved how his fragrance filled my nostrils and the feel of his clothing against me felt so therapeutic.

"I'll be in town longer than he will. I will see you again," he said.

I smiled.

"You may not have to now, but one day you will have to choose or you will have to confess to him. I know who you are and I accept it, but will he?" Kich asked as he got in his car.

He was right. There would come a day when I would have to choose. Neither of them were really husband material, but I knew this type of affair would run its course. I don't think they would ever really share me.

Maybe we could have a Poly Fly life like Taz's Angels.

I laughed.

I opened the door and peeked in to be sure Zay hadn't woke up. All the lights were now off in the house. It appeared as if Cookie had went to sleep too.

I crept back into the bed with him and

snuggled underneath him. I could still feel Kich's cock imprint inside me. Although they both were a great size, Zay's was a bit longer with a curve and Kich's was thicker. It's like Zay went deeper but Kich filled every part of me. His cock rested in me so perfectly and I loved that Kich didn't use condoms so I felt it all.

I eventually dosed off to sleep and was awakened by Zay kissing me.

"Stori, Stori, wake up," he said.

"Yes, what's up. What time is it?" I asked.

"It's like 7, but I'm about to go back to the hotel room. We supposed to be going to the studio with Kich," he said.

I started choking on my own spit.

"Are you ok?" he raised up in the bed and started to pat my back.

"Yes, I'm fine," I said.

No, you're not you liar.

I guess you'd better head back then," I replied.

Let me tell you this was the most awkward experience in my life. It sent an eerie feeling up my bones just hearing him say Kich's name.

Did I really fuck them both last night?

Zay got dressed and headed back to his hotel. I finally headed to the bathroom to take a shower. I had a mix of my powerful orgasms along with Kich's spunk still floating inside of me.

I turned on the faucet and let the water get to my desired temperature before starting the shower. I was just about to step in when I heard my phone go off. I picked my phone up from the counter and it was Kich texting me. It seemed weird seeing his name pop up because he had been blocked for so long.

Kich

Come to me.

I just woke up.

Should I tell him I'm about to shower? He's probably going to tell me to shower there, but I want to shower now.

Come now.

I haven't bathed
since yesterday.
And you know I
had a crazy night.
Can I shower first?

My hotel is minutes
from your place.
Just shower with me
once you get here.

What hotel?

Be Live-Atlanta/Midtown.

8

Ok, omw.

I was always grateful for Kich's precision because I would've been at the wrong *Be Live* knocking on the wrong suite.

I quickly began to get my things together without furthering a debate on whether I was going to shower on my own or not. I knew it was going to be like beating a dead horse trying to get Kich to understand. I grabbed a small duffle bag and stuffed it with a cute dress, basic hair essentials, some sandals, my makeup bag, a few crop tops and tights. I packed some extra clothes just in case I stayed longer with Kich.

I grabbed my purse and headed for the door. One thing I loved about Kich was that I didn't even have to double check to see if I had my wallet or any cash because he paid for everything, every time. I would make sure I had my license, just in case I went through a traffic stop or we went to get drinks.

I made it out the house without Cookie or Kara even realizing I had left. When I made it to my car I opened the back door and I threw my bags in the backseat. I closed the door and then I jumped in the front. I cranked my car and started blasting some tunes.

Kich's hotel was a few exits up on the expressway and I got there fast.

I pulled up to Kich's hotel at *Be Live* and realized the parking was valet with a fee. I text him to get the room number to charge it to. After that I gave valet my keys and they pulled my bags from the car.

"Would you like someone to carry your bags up for you madam?" asked the bellman.

"No thank you, I have it," I grabbed my duffle and my purse with a smile.

I walked through the automated door and I was amazed. This was easily the most extravagant hotel I had ever stepped foot in. The colors all seemed to pop out at me. I immediately felt relaxed because bright colors always soothed me. It was going to be hard for Kich to get me out of his room.

I passed an awesome spa on my way to the elevator. There was also a full restaurant and bar located near the lobby area.

Be Live Spa

That's an interesting name for a Spa. I'm sure anything goes in there.

"*Be as live as you want customers.*"

I laughed.

Yea I'm sure that's what they tell them.

I knew I was going to pay that spa a visit later. It would be easy to talk Kich into letting me go there to treat myself.

I made it to the elevator and I pressed (P) to go to Kich's penthouse. Nothing happened. I pressed (P) again.

I stepped out and went to the front desk.

"Hi, I'm trying to get to the Penthouse but the elevator won't seem to allow me," I said to the receptionist.

"Your name please," she said.

"Vistoria Jefferson," I replied.

"Can I see your I.D. please?" she asked.

"Sure," I pulled it out of my purse and handed it to her.

"Ok, here you go Ms. Jefferson. Mr. Montel has been expecting you," she handed me a flat key with the letter (P) on it and Kich's names printed on the back.

"This time when you get to the elevator insert the key in the slot and then press (P)," she smiled.

"Thank you," I smiled and walked off.

I was a tad embarrassed that I didn't know that but I would next time.

I had never been to a hotel this fancy.

I walked back to the elevator and did as I was told. I entered the elevator and slid the key in the opening right above the numbered area.

I inserted it and hit (P). The (P) lit up in a blue color and the diamonds surrounding the letter all let up in yellow.

Gosh is all this necessary?

I made it to his room and as soon as I was about to knock on the door he opened it.

"Hello there. Come in," he said and motioned his hand back as to direct me into the room.

Kich was wearing tailored grey pants that hugged his crouch area. Kich's penis formed a bulge in the center right under his zipper. He had

11

on a white shirt button down that was open revealing his chest underneath. I loved how his bronze skin shone through it and I could see his chest hair. I looked him up and down and even lusted over his belly button. It was something about knowing it was a pivotal point in getting his cock deep in my mouth. I swallowed as I continued to undress him and admire his gorgeousness. I walked closer to him and we were now chest to breast. I took my finger across his full beard that he had grown and I pulled the end of it.

"I see this thing finally thickened," I said as my lips were pressed softly against his.

"I cannot wait to ride the fuck out of this beard," I bit him on the chin. It wasn't as easy as it used to be with the full beard but I still managed to get some skin in my mouth.

Kich pulled me closer.

"I will fuck you right here, right now in this entrance," he growled in my ear.

I knew he was serious so I shifted on into the room. He knew what I was doing. He hit me on my butt as I passed him.

"Still scared of all my antics I see. That's fine. You'll grow to love them," he laughed.

I decided to change the subject. I didn't like when Kich made me seem like I was some newbie to his lifestyle that was unwilling to try things.

"So, are you planning to have a party or something? I mean why do you need a suite this big," I asked.

The suite was enormous. It reminded me of a fully furnished condo that looked like it had the best interior decorator alive. The suite was located in the perfect spot of Midtown Atlanta with the city skyline welcoming you every moment you gazed out of the wall-to-floor windows. The morning sun peered through the clouds onto the city causing it to glisten like diamonds.

I walked farther into the room and examined the bedding. I plopped down to get a better feel of it. It had the fluffiest pillow top mattress with enormous plush pillows. I rubbed the back of my leg back and forth across the comforter. The goose down duvet felt like I was at a spa getting warm milk and honey massaged into my pores.

Kich knew how to be over the top with everything. The suite had a dining area, a full-sized bar area with bottles pre-stocked and stools for serving, an Air Bath tub with a separate over-sized shower with glass doors. In addition, there was an extra bedroom and bathroom for guest on the penthouse floor.

Kich by now had made his way to the shower. I could see him through the glass as the suds began to cover his body. I watched him for a moment before joining. Then I walked over and dropped my clothes on the floor and slipped the door open. He was facing the opposite direction when I crept behind him. He turned around and looked me in my eyes. I walked closer to him and rubbed his face. We just stood there as the water

13

dripped on the top of our heads. The water trickled down Kich's face and got trapped in his beard that was full of suds. More and more water fell clearing the suds from Kich's beard. It was if the world was spinning around us, the earth was rotating, the sun was shining, the moon was prepping to come up after the sun had set, birds were chirping, dogs were barking, grass was growing, trees were swaying as the wind blew, but we stood still. We were frozen in time and we were the only thing that existed. Kich wasn't the last man on Earth but he might as well had been. I would not choose anyone over him and nothing could ever make me want to.

"Your eyes," I said.

"What about them?" he asked.

"You have no pupil," I said.

"Everyone has a pupil Vistoria," he said.

"But you don't. I don't see one. Are your eyes black?" I asked in shock.

"You know my mom had very dark eyes. That's where mine came from," he said.

"Had? Is your mom still around?" I asked.

I had to use moments like this to pry because Kich didn't always talk about his family or upbringing.

"Yes, had. My mom seems to think her green contacts are her eyes when they aren't. Most people who see her and see me don't know we have the same eyes. It's been so long since I've seen her eyes I almost forgot we share that," he smiled.

"Are you and your mom close?" I asked.

I was trying to dig in Kich's upbringing to see if I could find a loophole in where his personality came from.

"Yes, we are very close. She's the sweetest woman I know," he said and rubbed my face.

"Oh wow, that's awesome," I said.

"Has she always been good to you?" I asked.

"Well there was that one time when I was little," he looked away.

"What happened?" I looked up at him with worry in my eyes.

"I wanted to go to Disney World...and she took me to Liberty Land as if I wouldn't know the difference," he laughed.

"Seriously," I hit him.

"I mean what were you expecting me to say?" he teased.

"My mom was a great mom my entire life and I'm just blessed to be able to give back to her all her heart's desires," he said.

"So, where's your dad?" I asked.

"Shhh!" he said and kissed me.

"You're asking so many questions and I'm ready to fuck you," he pressed his fingers into my neck.

I could feel his hand tightening around me and my air flow slowing down. My eyes started to water and he kept gripping. Although the water was wet all around me his grip was so firm that I could feel the dry imprint of each of his fingers crating into my neck. I began to grasp for air anyway that I could. He bit my lip then released his hold on my neck. I gulped as much air as I could into my mouth to stop my lungs from giving out. He then pulled my hair with his fingers deep in my roots yanking my head back. My neck was fully exposed and he brought me close and started to drink the water from my body.

"Who do you belong to?" he asked.

"You," I replied.

"On your knees slut," he pushed my head down.

I was now cradled under Kich's balls. He positioned his right leg up on the soap dispenser in the shower and balanced on the corners of the shower entrance. Kich didn't mind allowing the remainder of his weight to press on my face. I think he liked having his balls and ass in my face.

I stuck my tongue out and started to sop on his balls that were now dripping with water. Kich then shoved his cock in my mouth and I started to suck on it slowly and deeply.

16

"Look at me when I'm blessing you with my cock," he said.

"Yes Sir," I said as I released his penis that was engulfed in the back of my throat. I slowly pulled it out of its secure man cave in my mouth. I spoke as I held his shaft in my hand and balanced his head on the tip of my tongue.

"Did you look at me whore?" he slapped my wet cheeks.

I looked up and stared into his dark eyes that revealed his soul. I was falling deep into the abyss that was Kich.

"No Sir, I didn't. I'm sorry Daddy," I replied.

"You're so perfect. You make Daddy so proud," he said.

"Thank you Daddy," I said as I continued to work his cock in and out of my mouth.

"Stand up," he said as he pulled my hair in an upwards motion.

He then spun me around and lifted my leg from the back. He stuck his cock in me and started pounding my pussy. The shower was becoming slippery so I placed my foot against the glass door for a bit of stability. You wouldn't have been able to tell how Kich was deep inside me without missing a beat.

I started to clench my walls around him and he wrapped his arm around my neck and pulled me in closer. His speed increased and then I was instantly filled with his warm spunk. He started to slow up as my vagina filled with all of his gooeyness.

He lowered my leg and I turned facing him. We started to kiss and let the water continue to fall on us.

We finally used the shower for its sole purpose and got clean. We stepped out the shower and grabbed our towels. I started to rub the towel up and down Kich's body. I squatted down and started at his feet. I slightly lifted the right one and dried it. I then lifted the left one and dried it. I worked my way up his legs and circled around to get the back crevice of his knees. When I made my way to his penis I patted softly to get the water off. I looked up at him and he was now looking down at me. The sight of his beard in this perfect lighting was taking me over the edge. I wanted so badly to ride that beard. As I fantasized I began to circle my left middle finger around my clit. I kept massaging his penis with the towel and pressing more as I felt him bulging.

"Did I tell you to touch my pussy?" he asked.

"No Sir," I replied.

"I like it. Sit on the toilet and let me see," he continued.

I stood up then sat down on the toilet and spread my legs.

18

I stuck my fingers inside my vag-hole and started moving in and out looking Kich in his eyes while admiring that beard. I rotated my fingers on my clit slowly. Kich walked over and let his saliva drip from his mouth and slither onto my vagina.

I circled it around my clit and thrusted my fingers deeper, curving them into the roof of my vagina. I could feel my walls clamping around my hand as I filled it with more and more of my fingers. I had now crammed my entire fist in my vagina as Kich watched me. He stood there with a hard on and a smile on his face.

As the pleasure began to take over me my vision became blurry and my head was rolling from side to side. I could feel my orgasm coming up. My moans got louder and faster.

"Oh my god. I'm cumming," I cried out.

My body was shaking from its release, and Kich pulled my hand out and dove deep into me.

"Ahhh, ahhh, oh my fucking god," I yelled louder.

My body was exuding with fire and I was exploding everywhere. My orgasm was squirting and oozing onto everything. Kich released into me and we continued cumming together.

Then I heard the suite door open.

"Who is that? Someone has entrance to this place other than you?" I whispered.

Kich threw a towel at me.

"I'll bring your bags in here so you can get dressed or do you want me to send Melanie to the mall to get you something?" Kich asked.

"Melanie is here too?" I asked irritably.

"Well yes. Most times I bring her or Rico. I never know what I'll need them for," he said.

"Well we know what you'll need Melanie for," I snarked.

"Don't start that. You weren't complaining when she was making you squirt everywhere," he said as he left the room. He stepped back in to hand me my bag.

I sat in the bathroom making faces wondering who that was who came in.

I hope that wasn't Melanie because I don't feel like sharing Kich with her this weekend. Although we do always have a good time.

I was interrupted from my fantasy when I heard a male voice out there and not Melanie. I knew I needed to hurry up and get dressed so I could go investigate. I threw my dress on and put my hair in a poofy ponytail. I still had my big curly weave in with a partial leave out.

I came out of the room and looked around. I could see Kich sitting on one of the sofas but I still couldn't see who he was talking to. I walked in the room more and saw it was one of Kich's friends, Ralph.

You may remember Ralph from when he

dated my stylist Tierra. Well per Facebook that's over, it's canceled.

"Hi," I spoke as I entered the room.

"Wud up?" Ralph replied.

"Kich I think I'm going to go down to the Spa while you boys handle whatever it is y'all have going on," I said as I circled my hands around in the air.

I never really knew what Kich had going on and I only asked when he seemed to be in the mood for sharing...kinda like earlier. Most times I just let Kich live his life and I minded my business.

I walked over to get my key that was near Ralph.

"Oh, excuse me," I said as I bent down to grab my key and purse from the table.

As I leaned in I could feel his breath get heavier and grace my neck. I looked at him and he was giving me a look of disgust. I scooped up my things and scurried from the room.

That was awkward. I sensed he wanted to fuck me, but then when I looked up he was giving me the (I'm three years old and just now eating broccoli) face.

I walked down the hallway to the elevator. I hit the down circle button and watched it light up in a purplish, blue color. The elevator came quickly and I stepped inside. I hit the (L) button on the elevator and I was lowered down to the Lobby where everything was located.

I entered the *Be Live* Spa and was in awe of its ambiance. I loved the light blue and purple colors. It was so serene. I walked up to the counter and spoke with the blonde-haired receptionist with the sexy full lips. She had her hair straight and sleeked backwards. She wore a white vest that had *Be Live* written on it.

"Hello, I'm Sarah and how may I help you today?" she asked.

"What all do you guys offer? I'd love to get a massage, a mani and pedi, and possibly a facial," I said excitedly.

"Oh well you have come to the right place. Here, have a look at this and I'll get you started," she handed me a pamphlet filled with all of their services.

I opened the pamphlet and flipped to each section that had something I wanted for the day.

I scrolled my index finger down the page as I looked at prices and what they had to offer. I started looking at the facial prices.

Facials

Triple Shot (75 mins) $180

The Semen Shot (60 min-anti aging) $205

Deep Within (90 min-acne) $275

Release (75 min-anti-aging) $255

Well I'm definitely getting the one that cost the most since it's on Kich's tab. I don't think I'll be needing a "semen shot" from here I already had one.

"Out of curiosity, why is it called a semen shot?" I asked.

"Because semen has many nutrients in it for diminishing wrinkles, smoothing the skin, and preventing further acne," she smiled.

I guess she could see the shocked look on my face.

"But to make you feel better the owner just likes to play with names. It's not actual semen, but it is a replicated non-human dispersed form of semen," she continued with a bubbly smile.

I fake laughed.

"It's created to have the same effects of actual semen," she said.

Kich would bring me to some freak joint of a hotel. That has replicated semen for my face.

"Perfect, for my facial you can put me down for the D*eep Within*," I smiled.

Massages

The Ginger Base (105 mins-full body)
$285

Deep Throat (60 mins-head-to-shoulder
targeted) $135

Radar (30 mins-specific area) $80

Live (49 mins-targeted) $125

"For my massage, I'll take the *Ginger Base*," I said and continued looking at the nail care.

Nail Care

Hot Cumin Manicure $65

Foot Cuff Pedicure $80

Shellac Manicure $35

Hot Milk & Almond Pedicure $55

"Hot cumming? Is this like the semen thing again?" I asked.

"Not cum-ming but *kuhm-in*. Black cumin to be exact. The oil has very good restorative qualities. There's an additional section in the pamphlet for anything you want to know more about in detail," she said as she swayed her pointer finger back and forth for emphasis on each word.

"I love this spot," I laughed.

"Very unique. I'll have to be sure Daddy brings me here more often," I continued.

"So, let me guess, you'll have the *foot cuff pedicure*," she laughed.

"You know I think I'll enjoy this *hot milk &*

almond a little more," I said.

"Oh, and I'll take the shellac manicure," I added.

"Is that everything...Ms..," she waved her hand at me to finish her sentence.

"Jefferson. Vistoria Jefferson," I replied and handed her the pamphlet.

I waited for her to charge everything to Kich's room.

"Ok, now I just have to be sure he's added you on the list for allowed persons for purchases," she said.

"If not I can go right up and have him come down," I said.

"Vistoria Jefferson, you're on the list," she said.

"You know what I'll add one more thing. I believe I need a waxing. That one is for him," I winked at her and she laughed as she handed me the pamphlet again.

"Smart girl," Sarah said.

Waxing

Basic Bikini Wax $35

Brazilian Bikini Wax $75

Half Back Wax $35

Wax That Azz $125

25

"This is an easy one. I'll take the *Brazilian Wax*," then I handed her back the pamphlet.

"I'm done now," I smiled.

"Ok, well Julia will be your masseuse and she will lead you to your room where you will spend the next few hours of your day," Sarah, the receptionist said.

Julia was a petite woman with rosy cheeks and dimples that deepened as she smiled. She had her brunette hair in a messy bun.

I walked to the back of the hallway with Julia in the lead. There were incense burning that smelled of lavender and nag champa. Down the hall, it was about 6 rooms where customers were getting serviced. Julia and I entered the room. It was a small room with a custom massage bed in the center of the room. It had the place for your head to rest in and it looked cushioned from where I stood. There was white fuzzy cover placed over the bed area. The lights were a dim purple bouncing off the walls. There was a small white sofa sitting in one corner of the room. In another corner was a counter filled with tons of products. It looked like lotions, waxes, and different tools needed for the services.

"You can place your clothing in this complimentary gift bag for now. For the massage, I will need you to strip all the way down and get under the cover placed on the massage bed. For your waxing and facial you can change into this,"

Julia said.

She handed me the bag and a white robe.

"Will everything be done in this one room" I asked.

"Yes mam. Everything but your manicure and pedicure will be done in this room," she replied.

"Well I'm going to step out for a second and let you get comfortable," she continued.

"Ok, see you in a bit," I said.

I quickly slid out of my dress and got under the fuzzy covers. It felt so good against my skin. It warmed me up because it was cool in the room.

I turned my phone on silent and placed it in my purse. I didn't want any interruptions while I was treating myself.

Julia came back in the room and I was naked and waiting.

"Are you ready," she asked.

I was already dosing off so her voice was very faint. I knew this massage was going to relax my tense muscles and put me deeper in my sleep coma.

So, this next part is me using my imagination on how this conversation went from what Kich told to me. Uhh...let the hating nigga syndrome begin.

27

Back in the suite, Melanie was helping Kich get dressed. As usual she was wearing skimpy shorts with her ass cheeks hanging out and a halter top showing her amazing abs and perky surgical tits. At the moment, she was bending down sexually putting his shoes on. Kich loved when Melanie wore those shorts because it was always enough to give a man a hard on the way her pussy slightly hugged the inner seam between her lips.

"So how long you been hitting that?" Ralph asked.

"Hitting who? I know you aren't talking about Melanie...we've all hit that," Kich replied as he hit Melanie on her ass.

"Ooouu Papi, you know I like it rough," she said.

Did I ever mention that Melanie was Dominican? She was raised in the States but her parents were born there. She spoke a form of Dominican-Spanish sometimes and other times she didn't. Sometimes she just merged them both together. Melanie was a feisty lil' sub bitch. I loved that under all that feistiness she was an amazing sub. You cannot imagine how much pleasure I get from riding her face until I burst all over that honey skin of hers. Here I go always getting off track. Let's get back to this hating nigga, shall we?

"Naw man, I ain't talking about Melanie fine ass. I'm talking about that lil' bitch Stori,"

Ralph continued.

Kich was drinking an Astoria cocktail with olives. He took a sip as he listened to Ralph.

"Watch your tongue brotha," he bit the head of the olive off the toothpick.

"Well you know what I mean," Ralph continued.

"I feel as if I don't know what you mean," Kich said curiously.

"I mean she gets around," Ralph said.

"Where is this going Ralph? Could you be more specific? I find that I am growing tired of this merry-go-round conversation," Kich stated.

"You know that's Zay's old girl," Ralph finally spilled out as if Kich was blind to this fact.

"You know what they say...one man's loss is another man's asset," Kich laughed.

"So, shall we head to our meeting?" Kich continued to maniacally laugh.

"Cute Ralph, I like it. I think I'll enjoy fucking her really slowly tonight to indulge in my guilty sin," he hit Ralph on the arm an exited the suite.

"Man chill out, I was just trying to help you," Ralph said under his breath.

Ok, now back to me.

"Ms. Jefferson. Ms. Jefferson. It's time to

wake up," Julia was lightly shaking me.

"I'm up. I'm up. Did we do the waxing yet?" I asked.

"No mam, I am not allowed to do that while you're sleeping," Julia said.

"Oh gosh I would've signed a waiver. I wish you had because I don't want to be awake to feel my vagina being snatched," I joked.

"But now that you're awake I can have Rama start on your facial and I can do your waxing. That is if you don't mind having two people on you at once," she continued.

I had a quick flashback of Kich fucking me in my ass and Melanie eating me out.

"Oh no, I don't mind. Two people is fine by me," I smirked.

"Are you sure? I will gladly do them both for you. This is just to conserve your time," she said.

"That's a perfect idea. Please bring Rama in. Thank you," I said.

Julia stepped out of the room for a second to get Rama.

They both came back in the room. I raised up and looked back so I could properly greet them. Rama was very pretty with dark hair and very dark eyebrows. Her eyes were brown and were the most beautiful oval shape. She had slightly full lips. It was the kind of lips that weren't too big but weren't too thin either. She had on her *Be Live* spa vest but I was dying to see what was under it.

"Hi, I'm Rama," she stuck her hand out.

I lifted up a little more and swung my legs around to face them.

"Hi, I'm Stori. I mean Vistoria. Stori is just my nickname," I laughed.

"So, which service will you be performing on me today Rama?" I asked with a mischievous look because I was secretly hoping she was doing my waxing.

"I'll be doing your facial today," she replied.

"Awesome," I smiled and plopped my legs back around and lied back down.

I will get to you soon enough Rama. I always get what I want.

"I'm ready," I said as I braced myself for the waxing.

I could feel Julia wiping my vagina and inner thigh area with a wipe. After that she went around my area with cotton. Then she sprinkled something on me that felt like powder and rubbed it in.

"Time to apply the wax. It will be warm," Julia said.

While Julia was prepping my vagina and

starting my waxing session, Rama was getting deep into my pores. I normally closed my eyes during my waxes because the sharp pain made me tear up but I didn't this time. I looked up and focused in on Rama's eyes. I could tell she was trying to focus on her job but I couldn't help it. I was enjoying having two women working on me at once.

I should tell Kich to arrange this for me. One up top and one at the bottom.

I tuned back in to Julia and my waxing. She added the waxing solution on my outer leg and worked her way into my inner pubic hairs. She added a thick wax coating on each section and pulled it up. Each time she pulled up a section of wax she firmly pressed her fingers over the sensitive area. She was almost done and it was time for her to wax my butt hole.

The pain of waxing eventually turned into pleasure. I loved the intensity of each follicle being snatched from my vagina causing my skin to turn red as my blood pulsated in that area. Only to have the hands of a beautiful woman rub down my tender spots with her gentle embrace. And to top it off I had Rama's pussy right over my head leaning in and massaging my face. This was the best spa day ever.

Julia wiped me down one last time with some kind of serum that soothed my skin even more. She finished with my waxing before Rama finished my facial. I still had more time to continue gazing into her beautiful eyes.

"Ok Ms. Jefferson it has been my pleasure serving you today," Julia said as she gathered her things.

"Rama will finish you off," she continued.

I get Rama all to myself now. How nice.

I couldn't tell what all Rama was using on my face but it fell amazing. She zapped my pimples and really cleaned out my pores. My face felt lighter already and it hadn't even been an hour yet.

I decided I would start a conversation to get to know her better and possibly invite her out to lunch with me.

"So Rama, I'm guessing from your name you're Indian?" I asked.

"I get that question and that assumption often, but no I am not. I am Afghan actually," she said.

"But you're named after an Indian Go…," I was cut off by Rama.

"Yes, I am named after a god from Indian culture," she smiled.

"Do you really want this back story of my name?" she asked.

"I would love it," I said.

"Well my parents were originally both

from Afghanistan and were refugees in India for some years before having me. So before coming to the States I guess they grew very fond of the culture there. So although Rama is a man's name they fell in love with what it meant and what he stood for so they gave me the name," she said.

"What does Rama mean?" I asked interrupting her.

"Oh sorry, I'm so intrigued," I laughed.

"It's ok. It means "pleasing" in Sanskrit," she said.

"I like it. I took a few religion courses in college and I remember that name. Rama was the 7th reincarnation of Vishnu," I said.

"Correct. My parents were in a world of rubble and we both know Rama is a god who instills peace and happiness. Although, I was born on American soil it was a reminder of where they were before they came here and how Rama's spirit had saved them," she said.

"Your name is winning for all kinds of reasons. It's pretty, it's unique, and Rama was so well-rounded from what I read about him," I continued.

"Thank you so much, you're so sweet," she smiled.

I looked up at her again and she was looking down at me.

"So, what time is your shift over today? I

have to get my mani and pedi done but I say after that we should hit the town," I said.

"That would be awesome. I get off at 4," she said.

"Perfect. Do you live near here?" I asked.

"Yes, I live very close," she replied.

"Even better you can go get dressed and we can find something to get into," I said.

My mani and pedi was another duel effort. It was done under the hour and I was out of there.

That was the longest spa day I've had, but it was worth it. Oh, let me turn my phone back on. I have been MIA for hours.

Kara Poo <3

Wyd?

Where the hell have
you been all day?

Whore!

You stink.

Text me back slut!

35

Tell Kich to suck
my ass!

I was spending Kich's
money. Shut up slore!

Kich

I see someone is
Having a good
time at the spa.
My bill just flew
Up by the 1000s.

                              Daddy it was not
                                 by the 1000s.
                              100s...maybe :)

Does Daddy get
anything out of this?

                              I met a sexy girl
                                 that I want to
                                 have fun with.

A new play toy for
daddy? Good girl.

She's mine but
I might let
you watch.

I'm going to have
to get you back
in the Power Room
fast. I believe
you're becoming
too feisty for my
sub.

I'll always be
your sub Daddy
because I love
to please you.
Nothing will ever
change that.

I noticed I had a lot of unfamiliar numbers
in my phone which was odd.

(444) 912-7777

Hey what's up

(901) 888-2356

Wud up lil mama

(512) 333-5555

Shit wuts good

(922) 544-2222

Hi, it's Rama.

I ignored all the other messages and responded to her right away.

Let me save her number real quick.

Rama

Hi love. What's up?

I'm off work and
I'm headed home
now. I can't wait
to see you again.

Ditto! I'll probably
catch an Uber to
you that way we
can get as turnt
as we want and
no one is driving.

Sounds like a plan.
I'll send you my
location so you can
put it in Uber.

Great! See you
soon.

(512)333-5555

You there?

40

Why does this number keep texting me?

I had to start getting dressed so I didn't have time to text back but I would once I got settled.

I showered quickly just in case any access wax or scrub from my spa day was left on my body. I never knew how the night might end with Rama. There was no telling what we would get into.

I put on a sexy black dress that hugged my boobs just right and some black thigh-high boots with a thick heel.

I turned and admired my body in the mirror.

I look like Cat Women.

"Meooooww, quiiiissss," I made hissing and purring noises while holding my hand up like a paw.

I immediately got embarrassed when I realized I was in Kich's suite still and not in the privacy of my own home. I stopped and looked around to be sure I was still alone.

I hope Kich doesn't have cameras up in this room like he does at home. If so, this is embarrassing.

Once I came to my realization I got my phone and requested my Uber. I watched as the circle rotated until it had found me a driver. He was 2 minutes away.

41

Great.

I picked up my purse and double checked to see if I had my wallet and the room key. After that I headed for the elevator. I pushed (L) for the Lobby and waited for it to come. As I exited the elevator I walked out of the colorful hotel and waited at the outside entrance for my Uber.

I got in my Uber and hopped in the backseat. He was an Asian guy who was playing some awful music.

"Hey, do you have an aux cord?" I asked.

"Yes," he handed me his aux cord and I plugged it into my phone.

I played some pop music that would set the mood for my girl's night with Rama.

We finally made it to her place and I text her that I was outside.

In a few minutes I could see her on the curb looking around so I stepped out of the car and waved at her.

"Rama, over here," I yelled.

She ran over to the car.

"Hi," she said.

"So, we never really discussed what we wanted to do," I said.

"I'm down for whatever," she said.

"Well that's what I like to hear. We'll go to

42

my favorite bar. Great food and drinks," I said.

I looked over at Rama in the dark, backseat admiring her physique. I could finally see and it was very eye catching. She had a nice tight body that was still very sexy. She had enough of everything. Her ass poked out but wasn't enormous and her B-cups were pointy and plump. I realized I was undressing her with my eyes when she smiled at me.

"What?" she asked with the cutest smile.

"Oh nothing, just looking at this necklace. I love it," I touched her neck slowly.

We pulled up to my favorite bar and the valet guys all came to the car thinking we were parking.

"We're not parking guys. We're just getting dropped off," I said as Rama and I were getting out of our Uber.

Cirque was always well lit around this time with purple lights. The entrance into the bar was slanted upwards leading to the door. We walked up and showed the guy at the door our I.D.s. The thing I loved about Cirque was you could get good food, a bar, and a party vibe too.

Rama and I sat down at our table.

"I like the lights in here," she said.

"Yea I know. It's pretty cool," I replied.

They were playing a mix of popular rap

music and R & B. At certain moments they mixed in some old school too.

"What kind of music do you like?" I asked.

"What?" Rama said.

I moved a little closer.

"What kind of music do you like?" I asked again as I leaned closer to her ear.

"Ohhhhh, I listen to all music. I mostly listen to anything with a good beat because I love to dance," she said.

"Nice, any type of dance you like more?" I asked.

"Nope, I love all dance," she said.

"Where do you dance? I would love to see it sometimes," I said.

"I have an open rehearsal tomorrow, you're welcome to come check me out," she said.

"I would love to," I said.

I started looking at Rama just because she was beautiful and I thought she would make a good playmate for Kich and I. However, I was starting to see something more. I was starting to see a great friendship forming because she had a beautiful heart. I hadn't once thought about Kich or what we could do since she got in my presence this time. Her smile was captivating and her personality was soothing.

We laughed and we continued to drink and eat our mixed wings.

I had tried to ignore my phone for most of our date but I finally decided to take a few photos for social media.

Why are these strange numbers still texting me?

I tried to focus on Rama while I responded to these weird numbers that had been texting me all day.

You would think someone posted my number on Backpage or something.

I laughed at the thought.

(444) 912-7777

So you gone act like that?

missed call
(901) 888-2356

missed call
(512) 333-5555

45

(512) 333-5555

Damn lil' mama
you ain't gotta act
like that.

I didn't know who to respond to first.

(444) 912-7777

                              Why are you
                              texting me?
This Vistoria?

                              Yes, who is this?
This Eric.

                              Well Eric I don't
                              know you, but I
                              want you to quit
                              texting me.
Ok, no problem.
I thought you

46

was up for having
a good time.

                    You thought wrong.
                    Idk what kind of joke
                          this is but it isn't
                                      funny.

          (901) 888-2356

                          Who are you?

This Myles.

                              Myles?

                    How did you get
                      my number?

                              Hello?

So you wanna
meet up later?

I don't even
know you. Who
gave you my
number? Is this
some kind of
joke because I
don't find it
funny.

"Is everything ok?" Rama asked.

"No, it isn't. I'm sorry Rama I'm having an emergency. I'm going to have to leave early," I said.

I had to find out why all these men were texting me. I could tell that someone was playing a cruel joke on me but I didn't like it.

(901) 888-2356

Hello?

Who gave you my
fucking number?

Chill lil mama.
My boy gave me
your number. He
said you was down.

48

Excuse me? Down
for what? What
boy? All y'all got
me fucked up!

Take that up with
him then.

Who is him?
Who is your boy?

I know damn well Kich or Zay didn't do this. I mean I've talked to Kich today, but I haven't talked to Zay. Is Kich trying to gangbang me or something? This is not ok.

Rama and I paid for our order and I called our Uber.

"I'm sorry I tuned out towards the end of our date...forgive me?" I gave her a pleading look.

"Sure, you can make it up to me by coming to my rehearsal," she smiled.

"I wouldn't miss it," I said.

I tried my best to give her the remaining moments of my attention while we were still in the car. I started texting my mystery men as soon as she got out of the car.

49

(901) 888-2356

So you're not going
to answer me?

Can I come see
you? I'll answer then.

How about this.
You and all your "boys"
are blocked.
Bitch.

(512) 333-5555

So what you got
going tonight?

Why are you
texting me?
I'm blocking
all of y'all
so you might

50

want to just tell
me which one
of your dumb
ass friends gave
you my number.

Kich

Did you give
anybody my number?

Zay

Hey.

Hello.

Did you give
anyone my number?

Kich

Why would I give
anyone your number?

51

Anyone who wants you
has to go through me
first. As a matter of
fact I already told you
that. I'm not interested
in sharing you with any
man as of now.
Watching you and
other women is
my thrill. Is
something going on?

                    Men are texting me
                    and I don't know how
                    they got my number.

Oh Vistoria, you're
a beautiful girl.
Enjoy it. I'm
sure it's nothing.
Maybe some of your
followers found your
number somewhere.

Yea maybe you're
right. Thanks Daddy.
I'm almost back to
the room now.

I'll be in a little later.
I'ma finish up this
Meeting and go
catch back up
with the fellas.

How many "fellas"
are with you?

It's like 6 or 7.

Is Zay around you?

53

Yes. Why?

                                        Nothing. Never mind.

Doubling back
already are we?

                                        It's not like that.

You're never
satisfied.

                                        Kich do not start.
                                        I'm just trying
                                        to figure out if he
                                        is behind these
                                        random guys
                                        texting me.

Why would he
do that Vistoria?

                                        If he found out
                                          about us.

He's not going
to find out through
me. But frankly
I don't give
a damn if he does
know. He doesn't
even know how to
treat my Princess. He's
a little ass boy.

                                    You're right Daddy.
                                    I'ma leave it alone.

        I lied. I wasn't. I figured I would be nice to
the last guy still texting me since I had already
blocked the other two. Maybe I could get
something out of them.

Zay

Why aren't you
texting me back?

Did you give my
number out Zay?
I'm not mad just
tell me the truth.
Why would you
do that?

(512) 333-5555

Why you being
so hostel? I just
wanna kick it with
you while I'm in
town.

Because I don't
know you. Like

56

for starters what's

your name?

Justin

And where are

you from?

Men are such idiots. He didn't know that I
was only going to play nice until he gave me what
I wanted.

(512) 333-5555

I'm from Memphis
but I've been living
in Germany.

Oh cool, what's
in Germany?

I work over there.

Dope. So what

57

                                        made you text
                                                  me?

You fine and I been
checking you out
for a minute. I
follow you on
social media.

                                        So that's where
                                             you got my
                                               number?

Naw, Zay gave
Me your number.

                                                  Zay?

Yea he said
we should hit
you up. He said
you was a cool
girl down for
whatever. I mean
                    58

I'm really trying to

get to know you tho.

    He had given me what I needed to know. I blocked his ass along with the others. I was embarrassed and I was hurt.

    Zay you sure know how to surprise me.

    I knew at that moment Zay knew. I didn't know how but I knew I was exposed. My secret had been revealed.

Chapter 2

<u>Permission</u>

I sat in the backseat of the Uber contemplating my next move. My eyes started to water, my chest became tight, my face began to hurt. I felt as if I was going to have a panic attack.

"Mam, Mam," the Uber driver was trying to get my attention.

"I'm sorry. Yes?" I replied.

"We have arrived at your destination," he said.

"You're right. I didn't even notice," I responded.

"Are you ok Miss?" he asked.

"I will be ok," I said.

I didn't know if I wanted to go in at the moment and face Kich.

I don't know if I'm sober enough to drive home.

"I'm going to set a new destination," I said to my Uber driver.

I put Cookie's address in.

The entire ride back to Cookie's was a blur. I sat there wondering how Zay found out and when.

I mean you did just fuck them both 15 minutes apart so what do you expect?

I rolled my eyes at the thought.

We finally pulled up to Cookie's house and I jumped out of the car. I didn't want to be around anyone other than my girls. I knew they could bring me back to life because right then I felt like...

Yep, I feel like...I feel like...

"Bleeergghkkk," before I knew it I had vomited all over the welcome mat.

I scrambled in my bag to get my key and opened the door. Kara was on the couch watching TV.

"Cook? Where's Cookie?" I asked as I pulled up my dress to wipe my mouth.

"Somebody had a long night," Kara said.

"Yes, very long," I said.

I walked pass the bar area and into the kitchen to get a large cup of water to pour over my vomit.

I filled the cup up and thought about how a perfect night was ruined by Zay. I was so tired of him hurting me.

"Stori, Stori. The sink is about to overflow," Kara said.

I snapped out of my daze and turned the water off. I went back outside and poured the water onto the vomit. I watched as the vomit began to separate and thin out. I knew I was going to need more because it was some remaining on the step.

"Here I thought you could use this," Kara said while holding a large pot of water.

"Thanks," I said.

She stepped off the porch and poured her pot full of water and now all of the vomit ran off into the grass.

"Dude, where's your car?" she asked.

"I caught an Uber home. I'll have to go back and get it," I said.

"I've sobered up a lot since my vomiting," I continued.

"So do you want to tell me what happened?" Kara asked.

"Zay is done. I'm so done with his ass. I can't believe he disrespected me like this," I said.

"Oh lord, what did he do?" Kara asked.

"He gave my number to all his friends and they were calling me and texting me trying to fuck," I started to cry.

"I was so embarrassed. How could he do me that way?" I tried to catch the tears before they hit my dress.

Kara went and got me some tissue because my nose had started to drip.

"I don't see why you keep giving him chances. He's a fucking dumb ass," Kara said.

"It hurts so bad because I still love him. I never wanted him to know about Kich and me. Kich was a mistake and now Zay hates me," I wept.

"Kich may be a little weird, but he hasn't even closely drag you through the mud the way Zay has and he doesn't deserve your love," Kara said.

"You don't know how it feels. I try to get away but something always pulls me back in," I blew my nose in the tissue.

"I love Kich but I'll never be the only one in his life. I don't know how long I can take that. Sure it's exciting now, but when I'm 35 or 40 wanting kids then what about then? Will it be funny then?" I said.

"Stori who says you'll end up with either one of them?" Kara said.

"I am trapped and I feel like I can't get out," I cried.

"Kich isn't going to let me go until he finds something that excites him more. Then I'll be a Melanie. If Zay and I could get right we could have the "American Dream" you know. First child together, first marriage, and live happily ever after," I said.

My head was down as tears streamed from my eyes and I rapidly unraveled the roll of tissue in my hand. I would get a big wad and blow my nose in it.

"Nothing will ever be happily ever after with that dick head. And while he's torturing you I bet he failed to mention he fucked Tierra," Kara blurted out.

I paused as Kara spoke and my head spun around like an exorcist.

"Tierra....did....WHAT?" I said infuriated.

Kara looked away and moved backwards.

"So at what point did she have time to be fucking Ralph and Zay while being in my fucking face," I yelled.

"Stori...she's been fucking him since he moved back to Memphis," Kara admitted.

"I didn't know how to tell you and I thought y'all were done. You had left him and Kich alone. I figured you had closed the doors and it was no purpose," Kara continued.

"Bitccchhhhh," I said as I started smiling.

"So here I was feeling guilty. Thinking poor Zay," I pinched my fingers close together and poked out my lip.

"Oh he's good. He is real good," I said.

"But hey I guess I'm still wrong because Tierra isn't my bestie. Just a friend I've had since college you know, my personal hair stylist when I lived in Memphis," I laughed some more.

"Wheeww, god I dodged a bullet. I dodged a fucking bullet," I said.

"Ha ha haaaah haha....fuck me. Revenge is sweet. Revenge is a dish better served cold," I said.

"Stori what are you going to do?" Kara asked.

"You can mark my words Kara. That was the last tear you will ever see fall for Varus Xavier Phillips," I said.

I put on my big girl draws and headed back to my room. I looked down at my phone and saw that it was about to die so I pulled my charger out of my purse. I looked to see if I had any text messages and I didn't. I figured Kich must've been having a good time because I hadn't been summoned back. Which was fine by me I decided I would sleep at home tonight and meet back up with him tomorrow.

I staggered in the bathroom and made my way to the shower. I turned the water on as hot as it would go. I wanted to burn away my pain. The steam filled the room and it was like I was seeing clouds. I grabbed my loofa and lathered it up really well. I figured it was time to get out once my skin had turned all red from the heat.

I grabbed my towel from the wall mount. I lifted one foot and dried it. I sat my right foot on the mat next to the top and then proceeded with drying off my left foot. Once I had dried both feet I continued up my legs, then my stomach and arms. I swung the towel around and gripped the other end to dry my back and vag area off. I hung the towel back up and headed to the sink. I grabbed some benzoyl peroxide for a small pimple I saw trying to come up. I stared at myself in the mirror and admired my naked body. I looked at my curves from my boobs to my lower body and how my waist formed a coke bottle shape.

Who says you gotta be a video vixen to have a coke body shape?

I grabbed my waist and was proud of how nice I looked. I looked down at my feet and wiggled my toes. I smiled.

I sat on the toilet and thought back to the days I was celibate.

Being celibate wasn't totally a drag. It actually had its perks. I could talk to a guy and if it didn't work out I didn't feel used sexually because I didn't give him anything. I never had any pregnancy scares or STD scares because I wasn't doing anything. And most of all I wasn't engaging in any soul ties and connecting myself to men like Zay who only got pleasure in destroying me.

I allowed my back to sink into the toilet

more releasing any posture I was holding. I sat there for over an hour just thinking. I finally exhausted my brain and started getting sleepy so I headed to my bedroom.

I walked up to my bed and pulled the covers back and slid under them. My body thanked me for giving it this chance to rest and rebuild.

I woke up the next day and it was after 1P.M. when I opened my eyes.

I rolled over and pulled my phone off the charger. I saw that Kich had text me.

Kich

I see someone had
a long night. What
are your plans today?

Hi. Yes I did
have a long night.
I'm much better now.
I am meeting a friend
for her dance rehearsal
but that's it.
I can come over
after that.

That will be fine.

How many more
days will you and
your friends
be in town?

They leave today
but I am staying
a few more days.

Great! Ttyl.

I decided to text Rama to see what time her dance rehearsal was. I assumed it was later in the day but I hadn't gotten a real confirmation.

Assumptions always make you an ass so it's better to ask.

Rama (the beauty)

I had added that lil' nickname to Rama's name because it was going to be my pet name for her.

Rama (the beauty)

Hey Beauty,
What time is the
rehearsal?

OMG, do not call
me that.

Why?

It isn't true at all.

Oh psshh.
That is nonsense.

You are one
of the most beautiful
women I've ever
laid my eyes on.
And I give all
my friends nicknames.
That one just
happens to be
yours.
I can't make a
shorter version
for Rama as a
nickname so I
had to make
something up
myself.

You have me
blushing.You're
so sweet and
to answer your
question, the dance
rehearsal is at 4PM.

Ok great.
That gives me
a few hrs. to
get dressed. Text
me the address
and I'll be there.

Ok, great.

Can't wait to
see you.

I laid my head back down on my pillow for a second and then I bucked my eyes.

"Fuck! I have to go get my car," I hopped out of bed and rushed to the closet to find something to wear.

I loved Uber but I wasn't going to keep paying for rides when I had my own car sitting in a parking garage at *Be Live*.

The temperature was starting to change a little as Fall was approaching—as well as my and Kich's birthdays. Zay's birthday was in the Fall too but who gave a flying F U C K about that. He wasn't getting shit this year because he didn't even get his gift the year before. We literally had more breakups in our time dating than we did any good times. I was blind to it at first but his recent actions made everything more clear.

I rummaged through my closet trying to find something simple yet sexy to wear. I settled with some high-waist jeans and a crop top.

I grabbed a thong and a sports bra from my dresser and put them on 1st. I then put on my top and danced my butt into my jeans. They were snug putting on but they fit me like a glove. After that I grabbed some white ankle socks from my dresser and put them on. I decided to wear my nude Converse with my look.

I made my way to the bathroom to fix my hair and face. I put my hair in a top bun and put on very light makeup. Light makeup for me is just sprucing up my eyebrows, mascara, and a nude or pink lip color. I was happy that I kept makeup in my bathroom other than in my makeup bag that was still in my duffle at Kich's hotel.

After I was satisfied with my look I grabbed my phone and requested an Uber. I put in *Be Live's* address so I could get my car from the parking garage.

My driver was a woman who would be driving a Lexus. I sat on my bed and waited for the app to say she would be a minute away. I always walked to the door once they were very close. Once it said that I got my purse and headed outside. My driver was pulling up at the gate as I was exiting. I got in the back seat of her car.

"Would you like to plug the aux cord up to your phone," she asked.

"No, thank you," I replied.

She was a black girl with long, straight hair. From what I could see from the backseat she was thick too.

Since when do you fill out women's physical appearance as if you're going to date one?

I guess I had gotten used to filling out chicks along with Kich and his fetishes. Kich always had these erotic parties where anything could happen. You could rest assured if anybody was touching on me they had to be top of the line.

I started to look around the car and noticed the pockets on the back of the seats in front of me

71

were filled with snacks, gum, and bottled water. Uber drivers in Atlanta took their business very serious.

We pulled up to the hotel and I hopped out of the backseat. I realized I had a little time before Rama's rehearsal would start so I decided to go up to Kich's room since I still had my key.

I walked through the colorful lobby and made my way to the elevator. I placed my card in the slot and hit the (P). That was the only way you could get to that floor where Kich was located.

I walked out of the elevator and headed to Kich's suite. I crept in because I wanted to surprise him. As I got closer in the room I saw Kich laid out on the sofa with Melanie's head in between his legs. He saw me as I rolled my eyes and smiled.

I sat down on the bed and kicked my shoes off.

"You're not watching," Kich said.

"I know I'm not," I replied.

"That's not polite at all Vistoria," he said.

"You walk in here while I'm being pleasured and you don't plan to participate," he said.

I looked over at him with my face tightened and he had his stern look on.

Kich had a look that could overpower any look I tried to have. My face immediately softened as I was weakened by his power.

"Come here," he said.

I slowly walked over. I realized at that moment I had been overstepping my boundaries as a sub and Kich was probably about to punish me.

"I'm sorry Daddy," I said trying to ease my punishment.

"What are you apologizing for?" he asked.

"Take off your bottoms," he commanded.

I took them off and started to take my shirt off.

"Leave the shirt and the socks on. I like to see you in that," he said.

Melanie's face never came up as Kich continued to thrust in and out of her mouth.

"Do you want me to leave my thong on too?" I asked.

"Yes, leave the thong," he said.

"I want you to climb over Melanie and over me and come sit on my face," he said.

He reclined the sofa back a little. I did as I was told and I climbed slowly over Melanie. My pussy was dripping in her hair.

"Keep coming," Kich commanded.

Now I was near Kich's stomach and I continued to climb.

"Pause," Kich said.

He took my right leg and propped it up on the arm rest of the sofa and began to dig in my pussy with his hands. Kich knew I loved to be fingered.

I moaned out.

"Do you like that?" he asked.

"Yes Daddy, I love it," I said.

"Come put that pussy in Daddy's face," he said.

73

I crawled up some more and rested my vagina on Kich's face. I looked back at Melanie who was now licking Kich's ass while massaging his balls.

The situation made me cum even more. "Tell Daddy when you're about to cum," Kich demanded.

"Ok Daddy," I said.

I continued to rock back and forth on Kich's face. I could feel my clit swelling up with blood as the pressure was about to erupt.

"Oh Daddy, I'm cumming," I screamed.

It was at that moment I realized Kich was pleasing me and my punishment was coming.

Kich pulled me in his lap and Melanie jumped back. He shoved his cock in me and started choking me. He then pushed me back on the floor with his cock still in me and now he was on top. He was pounding my pussy.

"Now, let's get one thing straight Vistoria. I am the one in charge," he said.

"Ok," I said in between my body cumming.

"OK?" he fucked me harder.

"You say yes Sir to me you fucking slut," he said.

"Yes sir," I said.

"You have become so disobedient and you know Daddy doesn't like that," he said.

"Yes Sir," I said.

"Did you really think I wasn't going to punish you for leaving me and rolling your eyes at me," he kept fucking me harder.

He grabbed my neck and started to slap me.

"Fucking, disrespectful, dirty, fucking, whore," he said a different word each time he slapped me.

"Open your mouth," he demanded.

"Melanie!" he yelled.

"Yes Sir," she ran over.

"Spit in her mouth," he said.

Fucking asshole. He's gonna let this bitch spit in my mouth. Ohhh, I'm whooping her ass after this.

Melanie got ready to lean forward and spit.

"Melanie, make it nasty for Daddy," he said.

She smiled and I could see her collecting saliva in her mouth. She came and stood over my head and let her spit drip down into my mouth. Right after she spit in my mouth Kich spit in my mouth. Then he stood up and came all over my face.

"Keep your mouth open," he said.

"I want this cum to drip from your rosy cheeks into your mouth," he said.

Once he was finished cumming he stuck his dick in my mouth and swirled it around.

"Do not swallow until I tell you," he said.

I lied there with spit and cum in my mouth just looking at the ceiling. Kich moved in closer to me and spoke directly in my ear.

"You are mine Vistoria. I own you. I own your body. I own your mind. I own your fucking social security number. I own your soul," his voice was crisp and solid in my ear.

"If you ever think of leaving a state I'm in and taking your slutty ass to a different one...you better hope you were with god himself," he echoed in my ear.

"No swallow like the good fuck toy you are," he got up.

It was the thickest thing I had ever swallowed before.

I don't know why I thought he was going to let me off easy. I really thought he had let that whole *moving without notice thing go*. It was at that moment that I realized I may never be able to get away from Kich. The same way he preyed to get me he would prey to keep me.

I continued to lie there in the floor thinking about the intensity of what just happened. Kich had fucked me in that floor better than I had ever been fucked. The mix of emotions and my body erupting were all feelings I didn't ever want to give up. Kich had so many folders he kept his emotions in. I thought after sex on my car, sex in his hotel, and my full spa day that I had escaped punishment. It appears he was holding it all in until the perfect moment.

No bitch, your rolling eyes set him off and made him remember everything.

I tilted my head back to see if I could see Kich. He must've gone to the bathroom to shower. I was covered in cum and I had to go meet Rama. I got up and got my phone. I still had time to freshen up before her rehearsal. I hoped Kich would let me shower.

I walked to the bathroom and peeked in. Kich was in there showering. I saw him cleaning out his beard. It was white and looked like Santa Claus.

"Santa, can I come shower?" I asked.

"Oh, you're a comedian now," he replied.

"Come," he slid the door open so I could enter.

I took my remaining clothes off and got in the shower.

He pulled me closer to him and kissed me.

"Was I too harsh?" he asked.

"No," I replied.

"Oh really, should I do more?" he asked.

"I trust you," I said.

"So what does that mean?" he asked.

"I knew you were going to punish me in some type of way because of my actions. I was hoping I had escaped it but when you threw me on the floor I knew I hadn't," I said.

"Uhh huhh continue," he said as he massaged his soapy loofa into my wet skin.

"I knew that whatever you did it might be painful but I knew I could take it because you would never seriously hurt me," I looked up to him.

"I could be crazy but I trust you with my life. I know you would protect me from anyone including yourself," I said.

"Vistoria, I am insane. You're a fool to trust me with something so precious as your life," Kich

77

said.

"Well then I shall die a fool," I said as I laid by head on his chest and let the water run over my face.

"Moments like this do not save you Vistoria. The deeper I fall for you the longer you will be bound to me. I won't know how to let you go. I will hunt you if I have to," he said as he pressed his forehead firmly into mine.

"I will haunt you for eternity," he grazed his teeth against my forehead.

Ghostly

If this is a curse, then I'll be doomed.
If this is a nightmare, don't wake me too soon.
I deserve this, I deserve you.
Plague me with your existence, dangle your remnant.
I don't care how you're in my thoughts, as long as you're there.
Cold sweats in the night, I'm waking and looking at your side.
Don't leave me, don't hide.
If there's a price to pay for your love, I'll give my life.

Kich's passion was scary but it was beautiful to be loved by someone so deeply. I know Kich sounded extreme sometimes but I can't tell you how much I trusted him. I cannot express how connected I was to his soul. Kich felt like me and I knew that he could never really hurt me.

We finished our shower and I walked back in the bedroom. I put my bra on and stood there.

"Do you need me to get Melanie to get you some more clothes?" Kich asked.

"Ummm, maybe," I said as I looked at my shirt that was unwearable now.

Then I remembered. I had left my duffle bag there.

"Actually not. I just remembered I had extra clothes in my duffle bag I brought over yesterday," I said.

I found my bag and pulled out another crop top and I wore my same high-waist jeans. Except this time I didn't wear any underwear. My thong was ruined and in the trash now. It was stretched and covered in cum.

"I don't know how I feel about you going out without any panties on," Kich walked over and stuffed his fingers in my jeans.

I just smiled.

"What if your aroma catches some guy's nose. No one is allowed in this pussy but me," he said as he kissed me on my lips.

"Well unless I approve it," he laughed.

"You say that but I don't believe you ever will," I said.

"I kinda have. You keep fucking Zay without my permission," then he grabbed my neck and bit my lip.

"You're crazy. Can I go meet my friend now?" I asked.

"Girl or guy friend?" he asked.

"Girl...my friend Rama. I mentioned her to you earlier," I said.

"Oh yes, the dancer. Well go on. I want you to come back here afterwards. You're staying with me," he said.

"Whatever you want Daddy," I said.

I kissed him one last time and then I collected my things so I could go to Rama's dance rehearsal.

I made my way to the elevator and through the lobby. I exited to the parking garage area and went over to the valet parking booth. It was a nice booth that had a TV area and a place they could sit when they weren't parking and picking up cars.

I tapped on the window.

"Hello," I said.

"Yes mam, how can we help you?" one of the gentlemen asked.

He was a very handsome chocolate guy with a very strong physique. He looked like he weighed 230 pounds of pure muscles. His muscles had muscles.

All of the valet guys were dressed in black suits with white collars. It reminded me of the

Peabody back home. However, Mr. Muscles was dressed down in jeans and a white V-neck.

"I need to get the vehicle for the Penthouse," I gave them my room key and he swiped it on some machine.

I guess it was to show if I owed anything or to be sure it was an authentic key.

"Ok mam, I see you're staying a few more days. I hope you've enjoyed your visit so far. I will buzz the other booth to have them bring yours around now," he said.

"Ohhh, so there are two booths?" I asked.

"Yes mam, we don't like to keep our customers waiting for us to run over to the garage all the time. So we try to be sure each station has at least 3 workers in it at all times to help business run more smoothly," he said.

"That's a great idea. More hotels should do that," I said.

"Well thank you. I was glad when Be Live chose to partner with my valet company," he laughed.

"Oh so you own the valet company? That's awesome. I love seeing men of color owning businesses," I smiled.

"Thank you, thank you. So how has your stay been so far. I hope you've enjoyed it. This is a great hotel so I'm sure you've experienced nothing but the best," he slightly bit his lip and gazed deeply at me.

I could feel the chemistry lock and my vagina walls clench.

I swallowed.

"Well that is true. I have definitely had an awesome experience here so far," I said.

He smiled.

"And here is your jeep pulling up right now Ms. Jefferson," he said.

"How did you know my name?" I asked.

"Oh yea, duh. It's associated with the key," I said.

"Yes mam," he said as he opened my door for me.

"I didn't get your name," I looked back up at him and our eyes locked again.

"It's Malroy. But most people just call me Roy," he smiled.

"Well it was nice meeting you Roy," I smiled back.

"The pleasure was all mine," he said.

"Welp, alright. There you go Ms. Jefferson and you have a great day," he said as he closed my door.

"Gosh this hotel is perfect," I said as I pulled off.

I put Rama's dance studio's address in my GPS. It was 5 miles away.

Great.

I knew I was going to make it in time. I was excited to see her dance.

I pulled up near the venue and I started looking for parking. I always peeped out free parking before I paid for it. I pulled around the back and there was a parking area for the studio.

That always made me happy because parking could be such a hassle at times. I parked my car and got out. I walked towards the tall brick dance studio.

Rama (the beauty)

Hey, I'm here.

I text her just in case she was near her phone. I walked in the building and went to the receptionist desk.

"Hi, I'm here to see my friend Rama's rehearsal," I said.

"Sure, you can just walk down that hallway and take a left," she pointed.

"Thank you," and I turned around.

"Oh sorry I almost forgot to ask you to sign-in," she said.

"No problem," I smiled and pulled the clipboard closer to me.

I grabbed the pen.

Vistoria Jefferson

"Here you go," I handed it back to her.

I made my way down the hall and to the left to find Rama.

When I walked in she had already started dancing. I looked down at my watch and it was 4:05.

Gosh, I see she starts on time.

Rama was twirling in aerial silk. It was so amazing to watch her and to know her. I had saw this type of dance at shows and fancy clubs but I never knew the dancers personally.

The music she danced to was a mix of pop and hip hop. She was wearing all black and her clothing hugged her figure. She climbed the silks that opened up to form a pair to the very top and twirled upside down. She then let go and her body came hurling down and at the last minute she caught on to the silk and spun around and through one side of it.

Gosh, she's going to make me have a heart attack.

She did a split in the air and swayed from side to side to the beat. She flipped upside down again and slid towards the ground and moments before her head was near the ground she flipped again into a split.

I gasped because I was so terrified for her.

I realized at that moment that I had to use trust in all of my relationships and friendships. I had to trust that Rama knew her craft and each moment was pure entertainment.

After that I could relax and enjoy her art. I couldn't wait to applaud her once she finished.

For her next rehearsal she had a male partner and they did ballet. I always loved how closely ballet dancers could fit their bodies together. Her dancer picked her up and threw her body in the air to place her around his neck. She then leaned all the way back and they spun together.

His neck is really strong to hold her up like this. Ballet is like extravagant porn. Like if they did this naked that would be amazing.

I straightened my posture up and looked around as if someone could hear my vulgar thoughts.

Now why do you have to turn something so beautiful into a sex scene?

Rama's rehearsal ended and she exited the stage right. I waited out in the lobby for her to come out. I sent her another text.

Rama (the beauty)

I'll be waiting
in the lobby
for you.

Yay! You made it.
Ok, I'll be out in
a second.

Of course I made
it. I'm a woman
of my word.

I sat down on the sofa to wait for her. I didn't know what all she had to do before coming out. I looked down at my phone and I decided now would be a good time to take (the beauty) off her name.

I guess I'll just stick to calling her Rama. It's super cute by itself anyways.

Sometimes I would leave side notes by people's names if it was common or someone forgettable. Rama didn't fit any of those cases so I could take her nickname off. I liked it but she didn't so I wanted to be respectful.

Maybe she was raised not to be vain or care about looks.

"Hi," she ran over to me and gave me a hug as I was still pondering her life story.

"Heyy! You did an amazing job. You are really good. I'm so glad you invited me to your rehearsal," I said.

"Anytime. So you really liked it?" she asked excitedly while jumping up and down.

"Yes, I loved it," I said.

"Great, the show is tomorrow but I invited you today since this was free," she said.

"Rama I would've came either way. I missed some of the beginning of your performance. I may come back tomorrow to see it," I said.

"You don't have to do that," she said.

"I really liked it and I have a friend in town. He may want to see it too," I said.

"Oh cool, is it a girl or guy?" she asked.

"Guy friend," I said.

"Oh I didn't know you were dating someone," she said.

"Well no, I'm not. It's weird," I said.

"Why is that an issue?" I asked.

86

I mean I liked her body and energy but I wasn't sensing that she liked me in a serious way. She seemed like a good girl. But I've learned those are sometimes the baddest ones. Take myself for instance.

"No, I didn't mean it like that. I meant if you had a friend in town that you were dating I don't want to take you away from them," she said.

"Oh, no it's not a problem. Trust me," I said.

"He will be okay. I'm going back over there when I leave here," I said.

"Ok cool, well I have a lot of things to get done before the show tomorrow so I'll catch up with you later," she said as she hugged me and gave me a quick kiss on the cheek.

"Did you park out back? We can at least walk to the car together," I said.

"Oh yea you are right," she said and grabbed my hand.

We exited the building and headed to the back where our cars were parked. Rama drove a cute, fiery orange Mitsubishi Eclipse.

"Cute sports car," I said.

"Thanks, it was my 1st car," she said.

"Well you have done a great job of keeping it up. It looks great and I love the color," I said.

"Where's your car?" she asked.

"Right over there," I pointed to my Jeep Renegade.

"Oh nice," she said.

"Thanks, well see you tomorrow," I said as

I headed to my vehicle.

    I text Kich once I got back to my jeep.

Kich

> I'll be there in
> a few minutes.
> I'm leaving the dance
> studio now.

Ok, I'll be in the hotel
a little later. Order
room service, strippers,
or whatever you want
to keep you occupied
but I want you there
when I get back in the
room.

> Yes Sir.

    I knew I had better followed instructions because I still wasn't out of the dog house just yet. I left the studio and pulled back up to valet. I pulled up on the curve and got out.

"You're still here," I said to Malroy.
"Yes mam, I was waiting for you," he said.
"Is that so?" I smiled.
"What time are you leaving here?" I asked.
"Now since you're here," he said.
"I would like to take you to the bar to have

a drink, if that's ok with you," he said.

"Well sure I have some time," I said.

He gave my keys to another worker and we walked in the hotel towards the bar.

We sat down at the bar area.

"What can I get you today my lady?" the bartender asked.

"I'll take a...," I paused.

Margarita or a mixed drink if you ain't tryna fuck Stori. If you tryna lay this handsome chocolate man then go straight for the Goose.

I looked back at him looking like a mix between Morris Chestnut and Lance Gross.

"I'll start with two Grey Goose shots," I smiled.

"Oh and can I have two limes to go with that as well," I continued.

He had the Henny.

In moments I was laughing and free.

"So I don't want to mislead you. I am staying in the Penthouse with my friend, who's a guy," I admitted.

"I know. It's my job to know. But it also isn't my business. I'm ok if his presence stops you from doing anything. I like you. I like your smile and I just wanted to be in your presence a little longer," he said.

I leaned in closer to him.

"Do you want to fuck me?" I asked.

He paused for a moment.

"Is this a trick question?" he asked.

"My pussy is all wet and I'd love to feel

you deep inside me," I continued.

"You make me want to take you home right now," he said.

Then I thought. I had told Kich I would be there when he came in.

"Give me one second," I picked up my phone to text Kich.

Kich

Can I have sex
with the valet guy?

Look who's being a
little slut on my turf.

You said I couldn't
do it without asking
permission.

You are correct.
I did say that.
Well how about
this. I am turned
on and intrigued
that you asked me
before doing it so
I'll let you. But you
have to promise me
one thing.

What's that?

Fuck him good.
I want you to be
a dirty slut while
you're giving my
pussy away. I want
you to tell me
what you liked
so I can use the
jealousy to fuck
you better than
him.

Ok Daddy.

"Let's go," I said.
"Go where?" he asked.
"Pay for the drinks. We're going back to
my suite," I said as I put his finger in my mouth.
"Check please," he said.
We rushed to the elevator and as soon as it
closed. I threw off my shirt.
"This is totally inappropriate right? I'm at
your job and we're fondling in the elevator," I said
as I wrapped my legs around him and he pulled my
titty from my bra.
The elevator reached our floor and we
rolled out. The entire floor was Kich's so we
started right there.
He tore my bra right down the middle and
my boobs just dangled in his face. He stuffed them
in his mouth going back and forth from the left to
the right. He then rolled me over.

91

"Take these fucking pants off," he said.

"Please do," I said.

"Shut up, did I tell you to talk?" he demanded.

"No sir," I said.

"That's King," he said.

"No, King you didn't," I said.

His large arms were so strong handling me.

He quickly got my pants off me and slipped his condom on.

"Take this fucking dick," he said as he spread my legs wide open and entered me.

"Ahhhh fuck, it's so big," I gasped.

I had found me a Mandingo.

"Damn, damn, it's so big," I said.

He put his hands over my mouth and kept going deeper and deeper inside me.

"Ride my face Dimples," he said as he turned on his back and put me on top of his face.

He pressed my pussy into his face and spread my ass as I moved around. His tongue was so thick and wet. It felt like a massage on my pussy every time it landed on my vagina.

He spread my ass some more and started spanking it over and over until I know my ass was red.

He then started spitting into my vagina that was already dripping from the excitement. He proceeded to lick back and forth from my pussy to my ass. Then he stuck his tongue so deep inside me that it felt like a cock fucking me. He slurped all of my juices into his mouth.

"You're a good little bitch. I like that shit," he said to me.

"I want to fill that pussy some more," he said as he scooted me back down to put me in cowgirl position.

I tried to wiggle my way down because he was so thick. My pussy had gotten somewhat used to his penis by now.

I bounced up and down and rotated on him.

He yanked me down into his chest by my hair and started biting my earlobe.

Then he spread my ass cheeks to the point where my hole felt like it might tear. He then proceeded to stroke upward inside me. I could hear my pussy making all kinds of gushy noises with each thrust. There was no need to clench my walls around his penis because he was already filling every inch of me.

"Ahhhaaahhha oh yes. Oh yesss, I love being bad. Do you like my slutty pussy all over you?" I asked.

"Yes I fucking love it," he said.

My body felt so good releasing the pressure on top of him.

"On your knees," he threw his condom off and came all over my face. He wiped the remaining cum off on my tongue.

"Look me in my eyes when you have my dick in your mouth," he commanded.

I licked around his head and swallowed it as I locked eyes with him again.

"I really want to make you mine," he said.

"Like I want this pussy whenever I want it and wherever I want it," he said as he pulled me off the ground to face him.

He kissed me in my mouth and picked me up. I wrapped my legs around him and allowed him to carry me from the hall into the bedroom area.

He laid me on the bed and just looked at me.

"You're an amazing woman Stori," he said.

"Well we probably should exchange numbers that way when you do have free time I can occupy that," he said.

I gave him my phone.

"Here put your number in there," I said.

He typed his number in my phone and then called it.

"I'll get yours from the call," he said.

"Ok cool," I moved a little to stop my vagina from contracting. It was sore.

My phone went off.

"Who's that?" I asked.

"Daddy," he said and looked at me.

"What does it say?" I asked.

Oh please Kich don't say anything out of the way.

He read it and laughed.

"Are you going to tell me what it said or do I need to get my phone myself?" I asked.

"It says for you not to bath until he gets here. He wants to see how slutty you've been," he

94

smirked.

My cheeks turned red from embarrassment.

"He's taught you well Stori and that makes me want you even more. It makes me jealous because he is in control and he's 1st," Malroy said.

He gripped my cheeks to where I was making a blowfish look.

"Your obedience is the sexiest thing a woman could have," he looked at me with so much admiration.

"You asked permission to fuck me?" he asked.

"Yes," I said.

"That makes me want to fuck you again," he bit his lips.

"I'm going to spare you this time, but just know I will be after you. I want you to be mine," he said as he kissed me on my forehead.

He exited the room and I could hear the elevator. He was gone.

I lied there for a moment and clenched my walls. My legs were tender in the corners from the pressure of being spread by him. Each relapse of pain made me picture him on top of me. I was so in a daze that I didn't even hear Kich come in.

I was still laid out on the bed clenching and smiling. I felt an energy in the room so I opened my eyes. And to my surprise there Kich was just standing over me, gawking at me.

Chapter 3
<u>Haunted</u>

"You could've said something and let me know you were in here," I sat up embarrassed.

"So it must've been good. Look at you. Still fantasizing are we?" Kich teased as he walked over towards me.

"You were quite the little slut while I was gone. Open up," he spread my legs and stuck his fingers inside me.

Kich got his phone and turned the light on.

"Oh damn, he was pretty big. I see he didn't cum in you. Where did he cum?" Kich looked back up at me.

"My face," I said.

"And where else?" Kich asked.

"And a little was in my mouth," I said.

"That's a good whore. If you're gonna give my pussy up you better make it nasty," he said proudly.

"So what did you like about it?" Kich asked.

"His head was really good and nasty," I admitted.

"And why was that?" Kich asked.

"It was very sloppy and he spit in my pussy," I laughed.

"And what else did you like? Make me jealous," Kich said.

"I think that was it," I said.

"Oh come on, you can do better than that. I come in and you're in wonderland so I know it must've been good. Tell me," he said.

"That's all. It was good sex but his head

97

was the most memorable. Everything else just fell along the lines of good sex and that's it," I said.

Kich sat down at the bar and started pouring himself a drink.

"You may go shower now," he said.

I got up and headed for the shower.

"He ripped your bra?" Kich asked.

I looked back at him to see if I had a piece on the floor.

"Yes," I said as I paused to see what his next reaction was going to be.

"Hmm...ok," Kich took a drink from his cup.

I proceeded to the bathroom before Kich could ask me anymore questions.

I started the shower and waited for it to get hot.

This is the 1st time I've asked Kich if I could have sex with someone. It was so spur of the moment but I wanted Malroy. Hmm...I hope Kich isn't secretly mad.

The shower had fogged up the bathroom and I was still sitting on the toilet thinking.

"Are you gonna get in or are you going to sit there thinking about your last partner?" Kich had come into the bathroom.

"I was letting the water get hot," I said embarrassed that I had been caught again.

I got in the shower and closed the door.

"I wasn't thinking about him. I was thinking about you. I don't want to be getting interrogated all night when you told me I could do it. Especially when you have new partners all the time. Melanie lives with you and I'm fine with that," I said.

"I'm quite aware of our arrangement. I'm just intrigued that's all. You won't be punished for this," he said.

"I want to compare your reaction from when you have sex with someone else versus when you have sex with me," Kich smirked.

I opened the door and stuck my hand out to touch his beard.

"Aww don't worry Kichy... no one can ever fuck me better than you," I laughed.

"Oh is that so?" he asked.

"It is," I said.

"Finish your shower, it's time for bed," he said.

I finished lathering my body with soap and I let the water rinse me clean. I stepped out of the shower and grabbed one of the fresh, white towels and dried off. I placed the towel in the basket underneath the sink and exited the bathroom.

Kich was already in bed under the covers when I came out. The room was kinda chilly because he had turned the A/C on. I rushed to be next to him so I could warm up.

"There's my girl," he said as I snuggled underneath him.

"So I feel like I haven't seen you as much as I would've liked on this trip," Kich said as he kissed me.

"What are your plans for tomorrow?" he

asked.

"Nothing for that morning and then later I am going to my friend's performance," I said.

"We're spending the entire day together tomorrow and I want to go to the performance too," Kich said.

"Ok," I smiled.

I was always happy when Kich took time to be normal with me. It sometimes made it feel like we were an actual couple.

"Go to sleep now," he said as he rubbed his hands across my eyelids.

I was exhausted so I didn't fight his advances. I allowed my tiredness to compel me and I dosed off into dreamland.

I slept peacefully through the night cuddled up with Kich. I awoke the next morning and he was still sleeping. I just admired his beauty as he lied there. It was rare to catch Kich in moments like this when he wasn't active. It was as if the moment he opened his eyes until he closed them he had something to do or a call to make. I saw through Kich that it does cost to be the boss.

I looked at how full his beard had gotten. I stared at how deep his eye pockets were. I noticed his nose hairs. I even admired the small freckle on his lip. I smiled at him as he lied there unconscious.

That was until Melanie came barging in the room with Kich's breakfast.

"He isn't up yet," she said standing over him with a thin gown on that was basically see-through. Her implants poked right through the shear white gown and she wasn't wearing any underwear.

"No, he's not up yet Melanie," I said.

"Well when he gets up can you tell him I brought him breakfast," she smiled.

"Sure," I fake smiled back.

"Would you like anything?" she asked.

"Oh no, I'm fine. If I want something I can go down and get it," I said.

"Awesome," Melanie smiled.

"Stop being a bitch Vistoria," Kich said as he rolled over.

I rolled my eyes and then quickly looked at him to be sure he didn't see me.

"It's not her you have a problem with, it's me," Kich said.

"I don't have a problem with her," I replied.

"I believe you do. You always have some snappy remark to make," he continued.

"Are you sure you're ok with this arrangement?" he asked.

"Well the 1st time you were inside of me I didn't know about any of this," I snapped.

"Ok so what do you want Vistoria? Do you want me to end it with Melanie and only be with you? If I do you're ending all your little rendezvous as well," he sat up in bed and started eating his breakfast.

"Well no, that's not what I'm saying," I said.

"So you admit you don't want to stop

having sex with other men?" he asked.

"No that's not what I'm saying either," I said.

"I understand your lifestyle and I know you and Melanie have been together for years. I want you to be happy and I don't believe that would make you happy," I said.

"Well in that case we're going to start doing some exercises. I believe the main issue you have with Melanie is because you haven't gotten to know her. So, every time you're with me I want you two to take some girl time together," he said.

"Girl time?" I made a face.

"Watch it," he looked at me.

"Yes, girl time. As a matter of fact. I need something to wear tonight and you do too. You two can go shopping and have lunch together," he said.

I was always interested in shopping so that tickled my fancy a little.

"Hmm...I'll do it," I said.

"Great, I'll have Rico pick you up," he said.

"Or we could just take Uber or I could drive," I said.

"I want everything to be my treat. I'll have Rico bring one of my cars," Kich said.

"And when did Rico get here? I haven't seen him?" I asked.

"He got here a little later and I haven't really needed him. But one things for sure is he's never too far away," Kich said.

Rico was the all-in-one guy for Kich. I

don't believe there was anything he could not do.

I went over to my bag and rummaged through the clean clothes I had left. I was kinda glad Kich was letting Melanie and me go shopping because I needed more underwear and something to wear tonight. Sometimes it's like he knows what I need in every way before I even say it.

I went to the bathroom to brush my teeth, wash my face, and take a morning piss. I sat on the toilet just allowing my body to empty itself as I played with the toilet paper roll. Once I finished I wiped and washed my hands. After that I headed back into the room area to find something to wear for this shopping trip.

I found a cute, loose fitting maroon dress that I threw on with my nude Converses.

"Are you ladies ready?" Kich said with a big smile on his face.

I had never saw him that excited. Guess he's happy his blended family is going on an outing.

"Ready as I'll ever be," I remarked.

"I'm ready Papi," Melanie responded.

I rolled my eyes. She always had a goody-too-shoes answer.

"Ok Rico is bringing the car around now," Kich said.

I headed for the door and Melanie grabbed my hand to stop me.

"Oh Vistoria, don't forget your purse," she handed it to me with a huge smile.

Kich was looking at me like a proud parent.

I could tell he was hoping that my response would be something well-mannered and not assholie.

"Thanks Melanie," I said and headed for the door.

Shoot me now.

"Vistoria, don't forget you're all mine after this. Melanie get me something fitting for the event tonight. You know what Daddy likes," he said.

"Yes, Papi," she said.

I rolled my eyes so hard that it hurt a little.

We exited the room and headed for the elevator.

"Wait up Vistoria. You walk so fast," Melanie said.

"Oh sorry," I responded.

"This is the 1st time he's let me go out with you. It must be time," she said.

"Time for what?" I asked.

"Time for you to know more," she said.

It was strange talking to Melanie. Majority of the time I thought she was just ditsy, but I was seeing a personality of her I hadn't before. This was also the most conversation we've had since I've met her.

We got in the elevator and pressed (L) for the lobby. We headed out the front door instead of the valet area because Rico had pulled there. I was a little happy about not going through valet because I didn't want to see Malroy.

Rico was standing outside an all-black Bentley with tinted windows dressed in all black. I loved Rico. His persona was always strong. He was very buff. He looked like he could be a body guard but he did so much more than that. I know his salary must be good because Kich gets him to do everything.

"Ricoooo," I said as I ran up and hugged him.

You would think my attitude would be a bit more resistant to Rico being that I last saw him when Kich abandoned me in that hotel room. But I never was mad at Rico. I understood that Kich's antics had nothing to do with him. Hell, Kich didn't even know he was going to leave me in that room when he 1st invited me over. This Zay thing catches him off guard. Sometimes I believe I'm the only girl to get Kich's boxers in a wad. Rico was like my big teddy bear and it was all love.

Now don't get me wrong, I wasn't a fool enough to think he wouldn't choose Kich over me if the choice presented itself. But that's where enjoying the moment comes into play. I never focused on the fact that everyone in my surroundings would turn on me like a pack of hungry wolves to protect him. Kich was Alpha.

"How you been Ms. Jefferson," he hugged me back.

"Melanie," he nodded his head at her as she got in the backseat.

He opened my door for me.

"Here you go beautiful," he said.

"Aww you didn't have to do that. But thank you," I said smiling.

Rico got in the front and turned on some low music. Rico knew everything. And by everything I meant life and how it works and everything concerning Kich. There is no telling how many secrets he has kept. There is no telling how many girls have come and gone. The thought made me shiver a little. I didn't ever want to think about a time where Kich wasn't in my life.

"So which mall do you ladies want to go to?" Rico asked.

"Lenox," I said.

"Phipps," said Melanie.

We looked at each other.

"Phipps is fine," I said.

"Lenox is ok too," she said.

We looked at each other and laughed.

"So how about I take you ladies to both," Rico was always the compromiser.

"What store are you trying to go in that you can't in the other store?" I asked.

"I wanted to go by Saks, Pressed, and Giuseppe for sure. All the other things I'm sure I could get from Lenox I suppose," she smiled.

"What did you want to get from Lenox?" she asked.

"You know...regular clothes," I smiled back.

"Those are regular clothes," she said.

"Yea for you and Kich perhaps," I said.

"Well Kich is paying for it so it could be regular for you too," she suggested.

"Phipps has a Belk," she looked and smiled

with the most reassuring eyes.

"Well there's the silver lining," I said.

I could tell she was trying to help but it wasn't going that well. Although I didn't know the 1st thing about shopping in those stores she named I thought I'd give it a try.

"I'll go in and see what you buy," I said.

"We can go to Phipps first Rico," I said.

"No problem Ms. Jefferson," he said.

We pulled up in the parking garage. Rico got out 1st and opened our doors.

"Where will you be Rico?" I asked.

"Just have Melanie hit me up when y'all are ready to go and I'll meet you at the car. I'll probably be around eating or shopping myself," he said.

"Ok great," I smiled.

"So where to 1st?" I asked.

Melanie grabbed my hand and whisked me through the entrance.

We took the escalator that led us directly into Belk.

"Do you want to start here?" Melanie asked.

"I'll look around but you can go ahead to the stores you wanted to shop in," I said.

"No can do. Kich's order are that we stay together the entire time," she said.

"Oh great," I said sarcastically.

"Well, let's start with you and Kich's items shall we! I have no idea what I really want. I just wanted something on my back so I won't be naked," I said.

"Ok Vistoria. In that case we can go to Giuseppe and get some things for Kich," she said.

I let her lead the way and I just started texting on my phone.

Kara Poo <3

Save me :(

What are you
doing girl?

Kich is making
me go shopping
with girl-Melanie.

The cutie with
the booty.

Uhh, spare me.
She's so happy
all the time.
It just seems
so fake.

You're just a
bitch Stori
face it lol.
Bubbly people
always annoy
you.

That doesn't make

me a bitch. I just
feel like she needs
to simmer down
a bit.

Yea, Yea.
I feel like I
haven't seen
you in days.

That's because
you haven't.

Did you tell
Kich what Zay
did yet?

I've been
having so much
fun I totally
forgot. I gotta
tell you about
Malroy also.

See hoe. You
been with
the shit.

I have. My bad.
But I got you.
I'ma catch

109

you up.

Kich calling

"Hello."
"I don't believe you're following directions."
"What do you mean?"

I looked around to see if he was in the store. I didn't see him. I then looked to see if Melanie was on her phone and if she had told on me. She was talking to the sales associate and not even paying attention to her phone.

"I am following directions Kich."
"You answered your phone on the 1st ring which lets me know you had it in your hand. Which more than likely you were texting or on social media."
"I didn't know that was off limits."
"You're supposed to be getting to know Melanie and to see things from her eyes. How can you do that if you aren't engaging with her but you're engaging with your phone?"
"I didn't think about it like that."
"Can you turn the phone off and please try to get to know Melanie. You might learn something."
"I'm sorry and yes I will."
"Enjoy the rest of your day with Melanie. Bye."

"Bye."

Apparently, this shopping visit meant more to Kich than he let on.

Maybe that's what Melanie meant when she said it was time for me to know more.

I turned my phone off and I put it in my purse. I went over and joined Melanie to see what she was doing.

"Hey what's up? What are you buying?" I asked.

"Getting Kich the *Runner's* with the studs," she held up the box.

"Oh yea, I know those. He wears them all the time," I added on.

"Yes and he purchases them a few times a year," she said.

"He buys the same shoe over and over?" I asked.

"Yes, he loves these shoes," she smiled.

"So while we were here I decided I'd go ahead and get him another pair," she said.

"Size 10 by the way," she continued.

"I'll keep that in mind," I said.

Melanie walked up to the register and paid for Kich's shoes.

"Now where are we off to?" I asked.

"Pressed. I want to get these boots before they sell out and then off to finish Kich's things," she said.

"Ok cool," I figured I might find something I liked in Pressed.

111

We walked to Pressed and went straight to the boot section once we got there. Melanie asked for the *Tie Up Transparent* boots in black. They were really cute. The sides of the boot were clear and they had laces in the front. I asked to try on the *Clear It Up* boots, which were basically a boot to your calf that was clear with a clear heel to match. It had a back zipper and was pointy toe. I figured I could pair it with a dress or something edgy for tonight. We both ended up getting the boot we had tried on.

"I'm glad I came in here," I said.

"See, stick with me girl and I'ma hook you up," she said.

"Now let's go in Saks so we can get Kich's favorite V-necks," she said.

We didn't spend much time in Saks. Melanie showed me which V-necks Kich liked and we were out.

"I still need something to wear with my boots," I said.

I ended up finding a cute non-designer dress from one of the stores in Phipps. It was a jean dress with a deep V-neck and a right thigh split. The jean was acid washed. I loved it and it fit my body well.

"So what about jeans?" I asked.

"We didn't get Kich any jeans," I continued.

"Kich likes to buy his own jeans or have tons of them brought to him," she said.

"He doesn't decide on his jeans until after

112

he's worn them. And it doesn't matter how many times he's bought that same pair," she laughed.

"I'm learning a lot about his preferences today," I said.

I realized at that moment I never really took the time to get to know this side of Kich, but I was glad Melanie was showing me.

As we were exiting the mall Melanie turned her phone back on to message Rico.

He just so happened to already be back at the car.

"You're always around the same time Melanie so I figured you would be headed out soon," he said.

He got all of our bags and put them in the trunk. Then he swiftly circled around and opened our doors.

"Thank you," I said.

Melanie just smiled at him.

"So where do you wanna eat at?" I asked.

"Oh gosh, it doesn't matter. I'm in the mood for a really good burger," she said.

We ended up stopping at a restaurant that sold good veggie burgers because that's what Melanie wanted. They had parking behind the building so Rico pulled there. Melanie and I got out and headed for the inside.

The restaurant reminded me of an abandoned ship. The entrance was made of wood and it had those netted curtains built over it to keep bugs out. Which was always a smart idea being in the south. This area was very large and some people were eating on the deck area.

We walked to the door and the aroma from all the delicious food engulfed my nose. I could smell seafood, chicken, sweet deserts, so many good smells meshing in my mouth creating flavors.

Once we got inside we stood behind this younger couple. She was blonde and he had brown hair. She hung all off his shoulders with a cute flowy dress and booties. He was in a T-shirt and jeans.

They were a good view to watch waiting for the hostess to get to us. She was a black girl with her hair slicked to the back in a ponytail. She was wearing a white button down shirt and black pants.

"How many?" the hostess asked.

"Two," I said.

"Ok follow me," the hostess said.

"Would you like a booth or a table?" she asked.

"Booth," we both answered at the same time and then giggled a little.

Our hostess found us a booth and sat down our menus.

"Here you are and your server will be with you shortly," she said.

Melanie and I slid into our booth and sat midway on each side facing each other.

We both opened our menus and started to look to see what we wanted.

"I believe I want the seafood platter," I

said.

"This burger they have in here sounds delicious. I can't wait to try it," she said.

At that moment our server walked up.

"Hi, I'm Michael and I will be your server for today. Can I get you started with a drink?" he asked.

Michael was a cute white guy with brownish-blonde curly hair. He wore his white shirt and black pants as well along with an apron for basic necessities such as napkins, straws, etc.

"Yes, I'll have a water," Melanie said.

"I'll have a water as well," I said.

"Ok would you ladies like a lemon in those waters?" he asked.

"Sure," we both agreed.

He went to go get our water and we continued looking.

"Yes I think I'm sold on this seafood platter. It has a bit of everything," I said.

"Well you should definitely get it. It's the only thing you've kept mentioning. I'm ready to order as well," she said.

Our server by that time had walked back up with our drinks.

"Here you are ladies," he set each drink down in front of its owner and sat a napkin and straw along with it.

"Are you ready to order your meal or do you need more time?" he asked.

"We're ready," I said.

"I'll have the seafood platter and I want

115

everything. I want the butter on the side, the cocktail sauce, every side dish and every seafood that comes in it," I said.

"Ok I got ya," he smiled.

"And what can I get for you Ms. Lady," he smiled and gave Melanie a cute eye.

She smiled back.

"I'll take the veggie burger with the sweet potato fries," she said.

"Ok, I will go and put your orders in now," he took our menus and exited our table.

"Ooouuu I think someone's crushing," I joked.

"Not here," she said.

"Oh whatever, you know if you wanted it all you had to do was ask Kich," I said.

"Yes, but I did something a few years back without permission so my punishment was I couldn't even ask anymore. I can only be with whomever he chooses to pair me with until he feels I've paid my dues," she said.

"How did he find out? Did you tell him?" I asked.

"Yes, I told him. I felt bad afterwards. He threatened to leave me and said I didn't know my place," she said.

"Do you mind sharing what it was that you did?" I asked.

"I fucked Rico," she said.

My mouth dropped.

"You did what?" I exclaimed.

"Yes," she said.

116

"Kich had left us alone as usual and we had been turning up the entire night. I'm talking x-pills, shrooms, bottles of liquor," she laughed.

"It's shocking we even made it out of that alive," she continued.

"But we did and there was this huge rush inside of me," she said.

"So, Rico resisted me for a while. He kept saying *Kich wouldn't like this, Kich wouldn't like this*," she laughed.

"At the time, I did not care. It was like Kich didn't matter to me. Of course I was high as hell but I wanted revenge on him. I wanted him to hurt. I wanted him to feel what he had made me feel a thousand times over," she continued.

I swallowed hard because I was nervous hearing all of this about Melanie and Kich.

"Why were you hurting?" I asked.

"Ahh ha ha haha ha," she tilted her head and laughed.

"You think you have envy. You think you dislike me? It's I who envies you. I hate you. I hate you most of all. But I know I'll have to love you. Because if I don't love you, he won't love me," she said.

"None of this makes sense Melanie. I'm confused," I said in a worried voice.

She exhaled.

"I was Kich's first," she said.

"So doesn't that give you more rank than all of us?" I asked.

"Not exactly. Kich loves me. But I have to

constantly prove my loyalty to him because I was his 1st submissive but he wasn't my 1st Dom," she said.

"And it's because of this reason you and a few others have been placed before me. It's like that one time still haunts me," she said and I could see small tears forming in the ducts of her eyes.

"Kich loves you more because your his," she said.

"He broke you in. He showed you the light. He's your Savior," she said.

"You would've lived in a life of lies had Kich not brought you into his. You would've always lived on the mediocre line never reaching the peak of sexual hierarchy. Because you would've been too afraid," she said.

"I don't know about all that," I said.

"Let me finish," she said.

"Kich knows he can mold you in ways he has to work harder in molding me because I have prior knowledge and prior experiences with a different Dom with different preferences," she said.

"It's all just learning. You can learn just like I can learn," I said.

"And see that's how I know you're still learning. But you also passed his test," she said.

"And made me look even worse. He'll always love me but he'll never really forgive me," she said.

"I don't get what's the difference," I replied.

"My Dom had a free range rule. I could

fuck anyone I wanted as long as it was under his roof," she said.

"Ok Kich has the same rule," I said.

"No, he doesn't. You think it's the same. I didn't have to ask to fuck someone with my old Dom. He liked the spontaneity of it. He liked for me to release as I felt and with whom I wanted. All he asked was to know afterwards the details or for me to record it. He was more open in that way than Kich. Kich's rule is fuck who you want when you're not around him but it's not the same if you are near him. You must ask permission. It doesn't matter if it's in his car. In his garage. If it is Kich's property in any form. You must ask permission 1st. This is a rule that wasn't specified to me. So I didn't know that Kich would be so angry with me. He called me so many names that night. He calls me his used whore. His damaged whore. All because he says my loyalty isn't to him it's to my last Dom," a tear fell from her eyes.

"I don't even like my last Dom that much. But Kich doesn't believe me," she continued.

"So the other night, when I had sex with someone else in his hotel room I made him proud," I said.

This entire world was different to me but I knew I was getting more used to it because I saw Kich's point.

"In summary, Kich wants you to feel free but he also wants to own you. You're bound now. You can never escape," she said.

"Why do you think he wanted us to go to

lunch today? He wants to be sure you understand the laws and what you did last night so if you ever break it he knows it was out of disrespect and not ignorance," she said.

"But yours was out of ignorance so that's not fair," I said.

"He doesn't care about being fair. Let's just say I'm the oldest sibling so I'll get taught lessons you never will. The guinea pig of the family. The oldest sibling always gets blamed because the parents always assume we knew better," she said.

By now Melanie was looking deep into my eyes and gripping my hand.

Our server walked up with another worker. They unfolded a table and sat all the food on top.

He then passed out our food and silverware.

"Thank you so much," I said.

"Thank you," Melanie said.

"That's why you barely talk to Rico," I said as I cracked open my crab leg with the silver clamps.

"Yes," Melanie said as she squirted ketchup onto her plate.

"Kich wasn't going to fire Rico because it was my fault. I had come from an orgy type Dom who was intrigued by random casual sex with multiple partners. Kich only allows it if he's in the room or if you've asked permission," she said as she bit one of her sweet potato fries.

"Because the thing about Kich is at any party he has approved everyone in that house. I'm talking about STD tests, background checks, etc. No one gets in Kich's parties without going through all of this 1st," she said.

"I didn't my 1st time and neither did my friend Kara," I said.

"That's because Kich knew you weren't going to fuck anything your 1st day with your scary ass," she said.

I dipped my crab meat that I had finally freed in butter.

"I suppose you're right," I said.

"Now Kara, he almost had to get her tested on the spot because she was about to go in," Melanie laughed.

"But you came down and spoiled it for her after watching me and a few others going at it," she said.

"That was you?" I asked.

"Of course," she said.

"That was insane," I laughed.

"You know I could never figure out what it was about you. He's never picked up a friend's girl," she said.

"I don't know either. It's like he preyed on me until he got me," I said.

"That's my Kich," she said.

"So how's the burger?" I asked.

"It's delicious. It has quinoa, sweet potatoes, and black beans in it. Those are like my favorite veggie burger ingredients," she said.

"How long have you been with Kich?" I asked.

"I have been with Kich since I was in my early 20's and I'm 35 now," she said.

"Whoa you don't look it. I guess Dominican don't diminish," we both laughed.

"I was trying to find something that was similar to the black don't crack," I said.

"Well I have black in me too so that one could've still worked," she said.

"So you're 2 years older than Kich. Wait Kich was 18 when he first made you his sub?" I asked.

"You've watched him grow in so many ways. Ways I will never see," I said.

"Well we grew into this. It was nothing like that. Actually Kich got invited to one of the orgy parties and we clicked. So we started having sex more and more without any titles because I was still with my other Dom," she said.

"Wow, this is juicy," I said while dipping my shrimp in the cocktail sauce.

"I broke rules for Kich. A lot of rules. And I believe that's also why he loves me so much but he doesn't trust me," she said.

"But anyways, we've discussed all the things you're required to know at this level," she said.

"Yes I do believe my brain can only hold so much information at once. I've definitely had enough skeletons for today," I said.

We finished up our meal and waited for the server to bring the check.

"You ladies enjoy your meal?" he asked.

"Yes," we answered.

"Will you be paying together or separately?" he asked.

"Together," Melanie said as she handed him one of Kich's credit cards.

Kich gave all of his girls allowances to a certain extent. If you were well behaved you would get a deposit on your debit card. Melanie also had access to Kich's credit cards. A lot of times when we went out we used his cards for our purchases. If we were in his presence or if it was a trip he suggested like this we didn't have to use our own money. Our personal cards were for just that. He gave them to us for personal things we wanted. It was a way for him to always know we had money even when he wasn't around. He loved for his subs to be well taken care of. He had just started back adding funds to mine because I wasn't getting anything during my runaway session. I was grateful because well behaved deposits always looked nice.

Neither of us got a to-go box because most times it was pointless. Kich would be ordering food or taking us out again shortly and the food just went to waste.

We exited the restaurant and headed for the back of the building. Rico was out there on the phone.

"All done," I said.

No matter what information had been told to me I still respected Rico and I wasn't going to treat him any different.

"Y'all all ready to go?" he asked.

"Yep," I said smiling.

He opened the back door for me and Melanie slipped in on the other side.

It now made sense of why she always opened her own door when riding with Rico and how she didn't engage much. I guess she feels bad about what she did and doesn't want the wrong energy coming off. I mean it was the reason that she's been damned the broken whore.

I was happy when we finally got back to the hotel. Kich had said I was supposed to spend most of this day with him but it seemed like I spent most of it with Melanie. Rico pulled to the front and opened the door closest to the entrance. This was Melanie's door so she had to get out. She quickly moved past him and then I slid across the seat and exited too.

"Thanks Rico," I said.

We scurried through the lobby and I had my shades on I didn't want to see Malroy. I was hoping my shades could make me invisible if he was down there. I was on Kich's turf and I wasn't going to push it. We made it to the elevator without bumping into him. Melanie inserted her key in the slot and hit the (P) button. I was so happy to see Kich again.

When the elevator made it to the top floor I burst out and went galloping towards his suite. Melanie went the other way to the guest room.

"Daddy," I ran in the room.

"I see someone's exited. I should make you

go shopping with Melanie more often," he said.

"I had an awesome time," I said.

"Now you see why it was important for you to pay attention. I wanted you to make the most of this," he said.

"I did and I'm happy you sent me," I said.

"I don't dislike Mel anymore," I teased.

"Mel? Well look at that. You've given her a nickname already. I like it," he laughed.

"I missed you. I'm so happy to have you in my life. I want to be perfect for you," I said.

"You're already that. No one controls me the way you do. Sometimes I feel like I'm your slave," he laughed.

I kissed him and then he took over it. Biting and licking my face. His kisses never stayed in the lines. He was always trying to eat my mouth.

"You complete me," I said.

We lied there in silence and eventually dosed off. Luckily I had set an alarm for the time I needed to start getting dressed because I knew with Kich we could lose track of time. I shook Kich a little.

"Kich, it's time to get up," I said.

We had an hour and a half to get ready for Rama's performance.

"I'm up," he said.

"Ok, well I'm going to jump in the shower really fast so I can get dressed," I said.

I undressed in the room area and then I walked into the bathroom. I took a quick shower using my towel and loofa. Once I got out I quickly dried off and headed back into the room to get my clothes I had bought from the mall today. I came out and Kich was already dressed and sitting on the sofa using his laptop.

"How in the world did you get dressed that fast?" I asked.

"You've been gone all day remember? I already bathed I just had to put my clothes on," he said.

"Did you get your things from Melanie?" I asked.

"No, not yet. I'll get them when we leave tomorrow," he said.

Oh yeah, that's right they do have to leave.

I think I had gotten so used to him visiting that I thought he was here to stay. This hotel felt like home even though it wasn't.

"That's right, you all do have to go home. I forgot," I said.

"You know anything I call home is also your home," he said.

"Yes I know," I smiled.

I walked over to get my shopping bags so I could get my things out. When I bent over Kich popped me on my butt.

"Ouch," I said and smiled.

"Darn, all of that shopping and I still forgot to get underwear," I said.

"I say you just don't wear any. This should be a fun night," he smirked.

"Ha ha, you would suggest I not wear any

126

underwear on the night I'm wearing this dress," I held up my acid-wash jean dress.

"Actually it is now a command. No underwear and I'm going to love that dress on you," he said.

I slipped my dress on and bent over to get my boots out. Kich stuck his finger in my vagina.

"Kich," I turned around.
"Stop that," I said.

"Don't tell me what to do with **my** pussy," he said.

I continued bending over so I could get my boot on. I stood back up and wiggled my feet into the right boot. The next time I sat down to get the left boot and slid it on my foot.

"See how fast you learn," he joked.

"You're so funny," I teased him and made a silly face.

I actually didn't mind Kich touching me. Actually, I loved when he touched me. Every time in every way. I just knew that if he kept touching me I would be late for Rama's show and I didn't want that.

I stood up and looked at myself in the body mirror located in the room. I liked how the dress fit my curves and high the clear boots added to the sexiness of it yet kept it chic. Kich came up behind me while I looked at myself in the mirror.

"Perfect," he said and pressed his package into the back of my butt. He then kissed slowly on my neck.

"I have to go do my makeup," I whined.

"I want to tear you apart right here and now but I will wait until later," he said.

"Thank you Daddy," I said.

I was surprised he was letting me off the hook. He usually would have bent me over and we would be going at it by now.

I went in the bathroom and pulled out my makeup. I put my primer on first and then I put concealer on areas that had any dark marks. After that I contoured my face to look like tribal markings. I had light and dark concealer on my nose, forehead, and cheeks. After that I blended everything in and added a little powder to it. I filled my eyebrows in some and added a red lip. I was looking fierce. I sprayed my face to set it and then I was done with my makeup. I added my powder and my lip color to my purse just in case I needed to spruce up.

For my hair I just made my curls really big and full with mousse.

"I'm ready Daddy," I walked out of the bathroom and did a pose at the door.

"You look ravishing," he said.

"Thank you," I smiled.

"Are we driving or is Rico taking us?" I asked.

"I'm going to have Rico take us," he said.

We exited the suite and made our way to the elevator. I hit (L) for the lobby area. Kich walked out of the elevator before me. He was holding my right hand as I trailed behind him. I was scrolling on my phone with my left hand and I

128

looked up. Malroy was walking into the hotel with a red polo shirt and jeans looking dead at me.

I put my head back down immediately and I didn't look up until we had exited the hotel.

"Was that your little friend? Or should I say big friend?" he asked.

"What? Why would you say that?" he asked.

"I saw him looking at you from the moment he entered the doors and your breathing changed. Your hands became sweaty," he said.

"That doesn't mean anything," I said.

"You didn't answer my question. I don't like asking you things twice," he said.

"Yes, it was him. The large guy in the red shirt," I said.

I thought about Melanie so I tried to explain.

"I was on my phone and I just happened to look up and I saw him. I looked away once I realized it was him. I didn't stare or give any signals," I said.

"Oh I know you didn't. You're smarter than that," he said.

Rico was waiting out front. He was driving an all-black Hummer this time. It too had tinted windows.

He opened my door for me.

"Mam," he said as he held it open.

"Thanks Rico," I smiled.

He went to the other side and opened Kich's for him as well.

"Sir," he said.

I sat next to Kich in silence hoping he wasn't mad.

Rico pulled off from the hotel.

"It's later," Kich said.

He climbed on top of me and raised my dress up. He pulled his cock from his zipper and stuck it inside of me.

I gasped when he entered.

"Who do you belong to?" he asked in between pumps.

"You, I belong to you," he said.

"Don't you ever forget that," he bit my neck and then he came inside me.

It was the quickest quickie we had ever had. I feel like he did it to prove a point and not for pleasure. Either way it was the passion that set my body on fire. I loved how he switched it up on me.

As I said before, Rico knew all the secrets. This one in particular was nothing new.

"Are there any napkins in this vehicle. I have a large amount of cum inside me and I don't have panties on. This is a disaster waiting to happen," I said.

"I'll give it to you right before we get out of the car. I want it to sit in you for a while," he said.

I wanted to roll my eyes but I refrained.

Once we pulled to the back of the dance studio he reached in the armrest and pulled me out a black handkerchief.

"Here you go," he handed it to me.

"Thank you kind sir," I said.

I lifted my bottom a little in the air. Next, I folded the handkerchief in half and wiped from front to back getting all of my and Kich's cum out. I then folded the handkerchief the other way and held it.

"Garbage please," I said.

Rico handed me a small, black bag to put it in.

"Thank you," I said.

Kich and I got out of the vehicle and walked towards the entrance at the front. I was twisting and still trying to feel normal after just having my pussy pounded in the backseat of his Hummer.

"Better?" Kich asked.

"Is what better?" I asked as I pulled my dress down some.

"Is it better since you no longer have my unborn oozing out of you," he came closely and spoke directly in my ear.

"Yes, it's a whole lot better. I'm just trying to walk right after having my walls spread a minute ago that's all," I said.

As we were entering the building there was a short brunette lady passing out programs. Kich and I both got one.

"Do you want to get a snack before we go in?" I asked.

"Yes, I'm starving," he said.

Kich was always hungry.

We went to the food area and got something to eat.

131

They had hot dogs, nachos, pizza, chips, and candy.

I got a hot dog and chips. Kich got pizza and candy. We both got a bottled water to drink.

After we had our snacks we headed for the viewing area.

"This is going to be awesome," I said as I looked back at Kich whose face was plastered in his pizza.

"Emmm hmm," he pushed out while stuffing his face.

Thankfully there were nice workers holding the doors open for everyone because I'm convinced Kich would've ran dead into it. I located our seats with no help from Kich at all.

"We're right over here," I said.

The theater area this time was way larger than the area Rama practiced in. There was an Orchestra level, a Mezzanine, and at least three more levels of balcony seats.

Kich and I had front row tickets. Rama let me get them for a discounted price. I paid for two just in case someone wanted to go with me. I was happy Kich did.

We ate most of our food before the show started. I only had a few chips and a piece of my hot dog left when the lights started to dim. Of course Kich's pizza was massacred but he had candy left.

The opening act was a hip-hop routine filled with Crumpers and all. I loved seeing their bodies erupt with the beat.

The next act was ballet with a live opera singer for music. It was very beautiful. Each performance was like 15 minutes.

After that it was time for intermission.

"I have to use the restroom," I said as I was getting out of my chair.

"And I'm still hungry," Kich said.

"Let me guess headed to get more pizza," I joked.

"You know it," he said as we walked down the aisles and into the lobby area.

"We'll I'll meet you back at the seats," I said.

"Sure," I said.

"Do you want anything?" he asked.

"No, I'm fine but thank you," I said.

I made my way to the ladies restroom. There was a small line leading out into the hallway. Each time the line got shorter the women closest to the door had to hold it open. I knew I was getting closer when the door was resting on my shoulder. I don't know why we didn't just let the door close. I guess it seemed rude and it also wasn't a way to tell if a stall was free with a closed door. Either way I was happy when I could finally get to the toilet. I entered the bathroom and looked at the toilet to see if there were any pee drippings on the seat. After I didn't see any I grabbed a few toilet seat covers and put them down. I sat down and peed. I took my phone out my purse to see if I had any messages from anyone.

I had one from Malroy. I opened it.

Malroy

You looked beautiful
today.

I tried to decide if I should text back or not.
Kich sometimes checked my phone. I didn't know
if this would be considered disrespect or not. I just
knew I didn't want to get on Kich's bad side so I
didn't respond. I also had a message from Kara.

Kara Poo <3

I miss you.
When are you
coming home?

Tomorrow :(

Why the sad face?

Because I already
miss Kich and
he hasn't left.
I wish he
lived here.

I mean he can.

He has the
money.

                                        True but
                                        he loves
                                        his place
                                        in Memphis
                                        with all of
                                        his exotic
                                        parties.
                                        Speaking of
                                        which it's one
                                        coming up
                                        for his birthday.
                                        I know
                                        you're in.

For sure,
the last one was
LIT!!

I paused on texting Kara back and finished
up in the bathroom. I got some tissue and wiped
myself then threw it in the toilet. I peeked out
between the cracks in the door to see if anyone
was looking back. After that I stood up and I
grabbed a piece of tissue and flushed the toilet. I
threw the little piece in the trash afterwards.

I exited the stall and another girl rushed in after me. I headed for the sink to wash my hands. I waved my hand under the automatic soap dispenser. Foam came out and I rubbed my hands together. I then waved them again so the water would come out of the faucet. Once I was done I grabbed a napkin to dry my hand and a napkin to get the door. The line must've died down because there was no one holding the door open.

I left the bathroom and headed for my seat. I figured Kich should be back by then.

When I got back in the seating area there he was. I could see the back of his head buried in food again. I just liked watching him in secret and admiring everything about him.

Kinda like he did me in the beginning.

The thought of that made me laugh.

"What's cooking good looking?" I said as I sat down next to him.

"That was a long bathroom break," he said.

"Yea we had a line," I said.

"Malroy text me," I said.

"Did you text back?" he asked.

"No," I said.

"Why not?" he asked.

"I didn't want to be disrespectful," I said.

"A text isn't disrespecting me. Text back if you want," he said.

"Yes, I'm your Dom and I am possessive but I don't want you to feel like you have to ask me to do everything. You're mine, there's nothing he can do to change that," he said.

136

"Thanks," I kissed him on the cheeks.

"He's going to try to take you from me, but he's going to fail," Kich said.

"Why so confident?" I asked.

"Because I know my power," he bit into his pizza.

"Cocky bastard," I said.

He laughed.

It was time for Rama to come on. The performance she was doing was the remainder of the show.

It was nice to see the part I missed at her rehearsal. Rama came out in an all-black body suit. She twirled onto the floor and the lights followed her with every movement. I felt like I was watching the closing dance scene of "Save The Last Dance" with Julia Stiles. Out of nowhere the ballet turned into hip hop dancing and then it merged from there. I was so intrigued by this entire show. It's like each preceding performance broke down the true essence of the genre while Rama came and summed it up. It was beautiful and it was breathtaking.

"The main girl is your friend?" Kich asked.

"Yes I said with a smile," I was so proud of Rama.

I smiled from ear-to-ear.

"She is so good," I said.

I looked at Kich and it's like his eyes were glistening.

"Is that drool I see?" I wiped his mouth.

"Be careful, I might get jealous," I teased.

"Her talent is so reprehensible," he said as he continued to watch.

She then moved into the performance I saw her do during the rehearsal with the aerial silk.

Rama ended her routine with a twirl jump into a curtsy and then the lights went dark.

When they came back on no one was on the stage.

Kich stood up and started clapping. Everyone followed his lead. The announcer then started recapping the dancers in the order of which they appeared on stage. Rama was the last name to be called and boy did the theater go crazy.

Rama was so beautiful smiling on stage.

After they exited from the stage Kich and I headed for the lobby area.

"I can't wait to introduce you two," I said.

"I have to tell her how glued you were. That was awesome," I said.

I waited in the lobby for about 10 minutes before Rama surfaced. Kich stepped outside for a moment to take a call because the lobby was crowded and noisy. Crying toddlers, chatter among friends, applauses from fans, all of that and an important phone call didn't mix. That's how it was with Kich. He always stepped aside from his busy life to enjoy life. I admired how he would put his phone up while he was engaged in someone's company or just out for some free time. Kich's motto was *Life is a present and it is our duty to be present.*

"Hey Beauty," I said.

138

"Oh stop it. I've told you about calling me that," she blushed.

"Well it's true. You're the most beautiful person I've ever seen. Well... next to me," I laughed.

"Does that make you feel better," I asked.

"Yes because that statement is almost true. Well once you take me out of the equation all together," she said.

"Stop it," I said.

I felt Kich behind me so I turned around. There he was lurking and breathing down my neck.

"I knew that was you," I said.

"Kich, this is my friend Rama," I said as I lifted my hand in her direction.

"And Rama this is my friend Kich I was telling you about on yesterday," I said.

"I do hope it was all good things," Kich said as he lifted her hand slowly and kissed it.

"Nice to meet you Kich," she said.

"The pleasure is all mine," he said.

"Can you excuse us for a second Kich," Rama said.

"Certainly," he said.

Rama pulled me off into a corner.

"Why didn't you tell me that your friend was Kich Mawni," she squealed.

"Oh my fucking god I feel like I'm going to pass out," she continued as she looked back at Kich.

"I dunno... I guess I didn't think much of it.

He's just Kich to me," I said as I looked back to him.

"Just Kich? He is not just Kich. He's THE Kich. Kich Montel turned Kich Mawni," she said with this dreamy look on her face.

"I take it you're a fan," I laughed.

"Of course, he wrote some of my favorite songs so when I found out he was coming from behind the scenes I was all for it," she said.

"Well I'm glad you got to meet him. This is awesome," I said.

"We should probably go join him again," I continued.

"Oh right...sure," she said as she pulled me back over.

"Sorry Kich. Just had to have a little private girl talk," she said as her eyes gleamed with excitement.

"So Rama, I loved the performance. The aerial silk routine won me over. Let's say I book you for my next themed party. I'm into masquerade and pretty much anything exotic. And that's you," he said.

"Wooow, oh wow. Really?" she asked.

"Really Kich?" I chimed in.

"Are you sure?" I continued.

"Which party exactly. Your birthday party?" I asked with a worried look on my face.

I knew where this could lead and I didn't know if Rama was ready to be a part of Kich's world. I didn't know if she could handle it. She was such a sweet girl. But I knew that Kich

140

must've smelled something he liked and when that happens he would not take no for an answer. Kich would write Rama a check then and there if it would make her agree.

"Stori, what do you think? Do you think I would fit in? You've been to the parties before right?" she asked.

"Well...you know. Rama...I think maybe," I looked up at Kich and he was glaring at me as if he knew I was going to say something that would make her say *no*.

"I think, that you up in the air doing your gift would be perfect. You won't even be able to pay attention to what's happening on the ground," I said with a very awkward smile.

"Ohh kay...well where is the party?" she asked.

"The party is back at my mansion in Memphis, TN. I can fly you and Vistoria out that weekend," he said.

"Well I guess it's settled. I'm all in," she said with a huge smile on her face as she hugged me tightly.

I was happy for Rama because she was happy but I was afraid for Rama. She was so fragile and inexperienced. Kich was going to turn her out. The bad thing was Kich didn't always keep every girl he turned out. It had to be something special for him to keep you in his collection. I didn't want Rama to be ruined. I didn't want this experience to haunt the rest of her life.

Chapter 4
<u>Live</u>

"So why her Kich? Can't you get another dancer?" I asked as we exited the building. I was walking on Kich's heels and talking fast trying to get my words out.

"Do you know how long it takes me to search and book someone of her caliber? This was like an open audition and she landed the gig hands down," he said as we walked back to the parking area.

"But Kich I don't think she's the type of girl for what you do. You didn't really go into detail about what the party would consist of," I said.

"And I did with you?" he asked.

"What do you mean?" I asked.

"Did I or didn't I tell you what my party consisted of the 1st time you came?" he continued.

"You did not," I admitted.

"Yet, you loved it," he said.

"I grew to love it," I said.

He turned and faced me.

"Vistoria, you know I don't like it when you lie," he said.

"I loved it," I said.

"So, you have to know I am great at picking my guest and my participants. Don't doubt me. You weren't what you are now when I first welcomed you. Rama will be fine," he said as he opened the backseat door for me.

"It's fine, I have it," he motioned to Rico who was headed to open it.

I climbed in the vehicle and sat down. I exhaled and put my seat belt on. I waited for him

143

to get in with me before I continued discussing.

Once he got in I looked his way and smiled.

"You're right. I don't know why I was worried," I said.

"All this time and you still don't fully trust my actions," he said.

"You're so right and for that I am sorry," I said.

"She seems like such a reserved and shy girl. I just don't want to ruin her," I said.

Kich looked at me with a confused look on his face. His brows raised and his cheeks tight.

"Did I ruin you?" he asked.

"Well no you didn't ruin me, but I've always had curiosity about this life," I said.

"And you think Rama doesn't?" he smirked.

"Well no," I said.

"Wait...does she?" I asked.

"I guess I don't have the gift yet," I said.

"Curiosity Vistoria. It is the only trait I need to see," Kich said.

We had talked so long to Rama that traffic leaving the studio had died down some so it didn't take too long to get out of the area and back to the hotel.

Rico pulled to the front and Kich and I hopped out.

"You want to grab some dinner from the restaurant?" Kich asked.

"Yes, I need a real meal now," I said.

144

We walked through the lobby and made our way over to the restaurant. Our hostess seated us and we waited for our server.

It didn't take us long to decide what we wanted after we had received our menus from our very round waitress. Her head was round and so was her body. She kind of reminded me of Ms. Puff from SpongeBob.

I had a Caesar salad and Kich had steak, potatoes, and asparagus. I also had a water and two strawberry margaritas blended to drink. Kich had just water. It was the cherry on top of an amazing day filled with Kich.

The restaurant had soft jazz music playing and dim lights. The chandeliers glistened above our heads. Nothing about the moment seemed rushed. It was peaceful and I was present.

We truly enjoyed each other's company. I sat there staring at Kich and recapping how he had unlocked me. I sat there mesmerized at how my life had changed so much under him. I listened to him talk about his business success he had while in Atlanta. I was so happy for him. These days with him felt like a dream. Although this was his last night in town it wasn't *our last night.* Kich would always be mine and I would always be his. He was always just a flight away.

"Are you listening to me?" he asked.

"Of course I'm listening to you," I said.

"So I'm happy that everything you wanted to happen this week came to fruition for you," I said.

"You're a very different guy Kich. You don't pretend to be someone you're not. You don't sugarcoat. You don't fluff ugliness. That's something that will always be admirable to me," I said and deeply sighed. Comparisons of Zay vs. Kich played in my head.

"I feel like that was a targeted statement. Did I miss something?" he asked.

I laughed.

"Trust me. It's nothing," I said.

"If it's nothing you wouldn't have that smug look on your face. So it's something," he said.

"I might as well tell you. Zay did some really foul things to me the other night," I said.

I saw Kich's jaw tense and his neck vein thicken. I knew I couldn't back out of the conversation now or he would flip it on me so I just continued.

"He had some of his friends call me and make sexual advances towards me," I said.

I sighed.

"There was one friend in particular who just wouldn't go away. Even after I asked him to stop texting me. It was him I tricked into telling me that Zay gave them my number," I said.

"Which one," Kich said as he placed his hands on mine glaring.

"Ummm...it was Myles," I said.

"Myles dumb ass," he said.

"Wait no, it was Justin," I said.

"I mean more than one text me but it was Justin who just kept going. He talked about how

146

he's liked me on social media and some more creepy ass shit," I said.

"Is this the same night you asked me if I had given your number out?" he asked.

"Yes it is," I said.

"You told me you were going to leave it alone," he said.

"I was but they kept texting me. I just wanted to know why and who would do something so mean to me," I said.

"He never fucking deserved you," Kich said.

I looked down and took a drink of my strawberry margarita.

"You know I get it was risky having sex with both of you but I still don't get how he found out," I said.

"It was Ralph," I said.

"Ralph?" I bit my lip and titled my head up to ponder who this person was.

"The one who was in our hotel room the other morning," he said.

"He called himself trying to tell me that you were messing with Zay. I didn't take the bait. I ever so nicely told him I would take pleasure in fucking you that night to indulge in my guilty sin," Kich laughed maniacally again.

This is where Kich proceeds to tell me what happened in the room with him and Ralph. I've already told you that story earlier on so you're caught up.

"So that's what pissed him off even more,"

I said.

"Wow, I didn't even think he noticed me. He always seems to give me the cold-shoulder when I see him," I said.

"That's because he wants to fuck you. He wants to see what is it about you that he hasn't tasted yet," Kich said.

"But what he doesn't see is he's a fuck boy and he couldn't dominate you. You would dominate him," Kich continued.

"Tuhh, I don't know about all that," I said.

"It's true. He's gossiping just like a bitch. He'll get his though. All is still good," Kich said.

I didn't know what that meant but I was hoping Kich didn't do anything crazy.

"Are you ready to head up to the room?" Kich asked.

"Yes I'm exhausted," I said.

Kich left a tip on the table and we headed to the room.

Once we got in the room I stripped and went to the shower. I turned on some slow music and let it play over the small clock and phone speaker in the bathroom.

I turned on the shower and let it get warm first. I waved my hand under the drizzle to be sure it was ready. I stepped in and closed the door. I was in there dancing and soaping my body. I was so into my shower I didn't realize Kich had slid the door open while I was facing the wall. I felt his body slide behind me and I got an instant comfort.

I turned to face him.

I let the water run over my head and into my face. I just smiled.

"You shouldn't have to worry about a thing. You should never have to feel like anything less than the goddess you are. I know you have ties with Zay and that is something you will have to free yourself from but his actions are inexcusable to me. I'm disgusted," Kich said as he rubbed my cheeks.

I just looked at him with an unassured face.

"You still hold guilt about it. Deep down he still has a hold. It may be small but it's there. You shouldn't care about what he thinks of you when he doesn't give a damn about what you think of him," Kich said.

Reflections in Muddy Water

Honesty I value,
Honesty is true.
Honestly I'm naked.
I'm vulnerable with you.

I cut myself open,
praying that you would see.
I thought that you would love it.
I thought that you loved me.

Tell me the truth.
Don't feed me your lies.
Don't give me bullshit
that's a flowered disguise.

149

You lie to make me happy.
You lie to protect my heart.
When truth is, you lie to protect yourself.
You lie because of scars.

Somewhere down the line
you told the truth and
got in trouble.

So you lied because of fear.
You lied because of comfort.
Your lies kept me near.
But your lies made me crumble.

Give me the ugly and let me decide
for myself.
Give me the tang on my tongue
it's my choice if I belch.

I no longer want half-truths
you mixed with the fresh
smell of timber.
The lies plastered on the plate
those cold nights in November.

My sacred moments I shared
because I thought you would remember.
Remember I always kept it real
you never caught me slumber.

I was clay in your hands.
You molded me in dirt like a potter.
I wanted to believe what I saw
but I was looking at reflections in muddy
water.

Kich was right. Although I allowed myself to embrace Kich that night he came over and Zay was in the house I still felt something deep down. There was a hold on me that I had to break from. I had all the facts in my face. Zay was a broken man who didn't know how to love me. Some moments I didn't know if he even tried. I think it was simply being human. I had been holding a secret and it was finally revealed.

I didn't know if I would ever face Zay after this moment. But as much as I hated it the one part that still felt guilty also felt the need to carry the blame.

Kich and I finally got out of the shower after a much needed discussion. Kich always knew exactly what to say to me. Kich always dug deeply into those areas I tried to hide and he would expose it. That's one of the reasons I loved him so.

I got my towel and I dried off my wet skin.

"Don't you want to lotion me up," I said as I rotated the lotion bottle in my hand.

"I will take that honor," he said.

I gave the lotion to him and spread my leg and arm like you see people do for a cop. Kich squirted a large amount of the creamy substance in his hand and rubbed them together. He walked closer to me and looked me in my eyes. I smiled and bit my lip. He then lowered himself so his face was near my vagina. He tilted his head and started rubbing the lotion into my lower body. He rubbed the tops of my feet first. Then he moved slowly up my ankles and to my calf muscles. After that he squirted some more cream into his hand and worked on my thighs. My body was tensing up and was at his beckoning call. I could feel my body exploding with each movement he made on me. As he got to my thigh area he would rub the lotion in and use his nails to trigger different sensations. I was standing there naked with my mouth agape just stunned. He strolled his fingers right between my lips and over my clit. I moaned a little.

"Quiet. Did I tell you to enjoy this?" he asked.

"No sir," I said.

He moved pass by vagina and wrapped around to my butt. He added more lotion and firmly massaged every crevice on me. He had now made his way to my belly button. He came from behind me and pressed his body against me. He then rotated his finger inside of my deep hole. I laughed because it was kind of ticklish. He rubbed my stomach and I could feel his chest against my back.

I exhaled.

"Do you like that?" he asked.

"Yes I love it," I said.

"Tell me what you like," he said.

"I like how I was just feeling your hands

152

and now I can feel your body against me. It's driving my senses crazy," I said.

He oozed some more lotion into his hands then he picked up my breast and rubbed them. I laid my head in the crevice of his neck and just let him touch me.

He slowly eased up to my neck with his hands. He cuffed them around my neck, choking me.

"Do you like that?" he asked.

"Yes," I said with what voice I could muster out from his hands around me.

He let go.

"I'm all done," he said.

He kissed me and walked out of the bathroom.

I stood there for a moment still replaying all of his touches on me. I wanted him to fuck me right there but I knew I needed to work on my submissiveness a little more. I didn't want the way he spoiled me to ever take away his power. So I walked out of the room and I just climbed into bed.

"Sleepy?" he asked.

"Yes Sir, a little," I said.

"Well go to sleep then my Princess," he said.

The more I thought about sex the more sleepy I got. It's like the massage was kicking in like liquor. It was slowly transferring through my body and shutting down my senses. I was going to have a good night's sleep. This was my last night with Kich for a while.

I closed my eyes and I was out.

That night I kept being awaken by dreams. They were dreams of heartache. I did not want Kich to leave me. All of a sudden the reason I moved to Atlanta didn't make much sense. Nothing made sense to me other than Kich but I still had my goals. I had made some strong connections with my writing career since I had been in ATL. I knew that Kich would take care of me but I didn't want him to. I always wanted to be independent and truly appreciate everything he gave me. I didn't want it to ever feel like an obligation. And maybe that was the whole girl power
I-N-D-E-P-E-N-D-E-N-T
movement speaking but it's how I felt.

The last time I went to sleep I had a dream I was awakened by Kich's tongue between my legs. It was like the dream was real. Then I realized my REM sleep had merged with real life and Kich was indeed between my legs. It was the most magical thing to be awakened to and all the more reason of why it took me 2 seconds to cum in his mouth.

"You just love making me weak for you," I said as he climbed on top of me and looked in my face.

"You smell like pussy," I said and kissed him.

"So nasty," he said.

I looked up at him and stared in his dark eyes.

154

"Something is on your mind. What is it?" I asked.

"Why won't you live with me?" he asked.

I exhaled.

"Well Kich it's not that I don't want to live with you I just have other things going on for myself," I said.

"You say that like you're undecided on if you're totally mine or not," he said.

"Living with someone is a big step and I like my freedom and privacy to a certain degree," I said.

"I would never take those things away from you. Do you know how big my place is? You could be on one side of the house and I would never know," he said.

"Kich it's not that," I said.

"Well what the hell is it then Vistoria?" he said.

"Kich can we not do this before you leave?" I asked.

"That's the point Vistoria. I don't wanna leave without you. Hell, I don't want to live without you," he said.

"Kich can you just give me some time to decide?" I asked.

"You don't belong to me," he said.

"Kich you're being irrational. It's definitely not that," I said.

"Well help me understand Vistoria," he snapped.

"It's like for me I was raised differently. I

know you see this care-free do what she wants but if I lived with you I would feel like I'm adding to my role. I would want to be the one going to get your Giuseppe's size 10. I would want to be the one getting up making you breakfast. I would want to be the one taking your things to the cleaners. And I just don't know if I'm ready for that as well as juggling Melanie. It's different," I said.

I sat up to think of a better way to get my point across because Kich didn't seem to believe me from his facial expression.

"It's more than one reason Kich. For instance, Melanie. That's her time with you. Her and I just got better acquainted the other day and now you want us all under one roof," I said.

"That's because I like for anything I love to always be close to me," he said.

"You're making this so hard and it's even worse to hear you equate it to me not loving you or me not being yours when I live for you. I'd do anything for you Kich," I said.

"If you had to choose Zay or me who would you choose?" he asked.

"I'd choose you," I said.

"Somehow that doesn't feel like truth to me," he said.

"I'd choose you because you chose me," I said.

"Is that it Vistoria? Is that the only reason?" he asked.

"No Kich it's not the only reason," I said.

"How am I supposed to believe anything

that comes out of this mouth?" he grabbed the lower part of my face clenching it so that my lips puckered by force.

"I can't speak," I murmured while he still had a grip on my face.

He held my face and glared at me. His chest was going up and down as he took deeper and deeper breaths. I just sat there with my face being squeezed looking him in his eyes hoping that he would see something deep in my soul. He must did because he let me go and sat down beside me.

"Do I scare you Vistoria?" he asked.

"No you don't," I said.

"Sometimes I don't know how to handle what you've made me feel," he said.

"We will get through it. We have plenty of time Kich. I plan to grow old with you," I said.

"The thought of leaving this city without you makes me want to kidnap you," he said.

"So tell me what I need to hear so that I don't throw your ass in the backseat of that Hummer and have Rico drive you to Memphis," he said.

By this point I was crying because I didn't know what to say to get him to calm down because nothing was working. But I didn't want to go. I wanted to accomplish more on my own before I agreed to be tied down in that manner.

"I don't know what to say," I said shaking my head.

"Tell me something Vistoria," he said.

"Why won't you let me choose you. You

don't want to be in something with anyone because it was forced. That's not real," I said.

"Don't you want something real?" I said.

"You're acting like I don't care about you and that's hurting me. I don't know what to do to get you to see it," I continued as I threw on my dress from the night before because it was the only thing I could find.

"I just need you to know that I'm madly in love with you. And it has nothing to do with me being with anyone else. I ask permission before I do anything," I said.

"But you didn't Vistoria. You didn't ask permission to leave me. You left me and I thought you were still in your house up the street," he said.

"So we're just going to keep going in circles because of that. Am I broken now? Am I Melanie #2. Huh? You just gonna find someone else and replace me too all because I made a mistake. A mistake tied to some shit you put me in," I yelled.

"I put you in?" he asked.

"Yes you get mad at me about Zay when you knew Zay was in the picture from the start. You knew what you were getting yourself into so why keep blaming me?" I said as tears poured from my eyes and my words dragged out of my mouth.

"Because I didn't know I was going to fall madly in fucking love with you that's why," he sat down on the sofa.

I just looked at him and stayed quiet. I had

seen that look before. I had no idea if I was going to be seeing Kara again. I didn't think I had did a good job of persuading.

I finally mustered up some confidence to speak.

"Real love is not about controlling every choice that person makes. It's about trusting that they always have your best interest in mind when they choose. I get it. I fucked up. I was scared. I didn't know how to handle you and Zay in the same city. I had to do some soul searching for myself. I had to see both of you for who you really were. And I see that," I said.

Kich lifted his head and looked at me. I could tell his expression had changed.

"So all I'm asking is for you to give me a chance. Just give me a chance," I continued.

"I literally feel my heart fucking bleeding. But I will grant you your request," he said.

"Thank...," I started to say before Kich cut me off.

"Do not thank me. And please leave before I change my mind. If I change my mind I'm carrying your ass to Memphis kicking and fucking screaming," he said.

I quickly got up and grabbed my purse with my keys in it. I scooped up my Converses because they were near me. I left my other clothes, my new boots, my makeup bag and everything else. I power walked to the elevator and when I got to it I hit the down button continuously until the elevator clicked on our floor. I hurried in and hit the (L) one last time in the *Be Live* hotel.

Once I got to the bottom I remembered I had to get my car from valet. I was hoping Malroy wasn't there. Then I realized I was focusing on what I did not want instead of focusing on what I did want. I tried to change my thoughts really fast but it was too late. Malroy was circling the booth looking at something on it. I tried to slide up to the window and request my car while he was on the other side. This day was hectic enough without having Kich follow me down here and see Malroy and kill us all.

"So you're checking out from the Penthouse," the flamboyant valet guy said.

"Yes," I said with a huge forced smile.

"Checking out from the Penthouse," Malroy came around the booth.

I rolled my eyes and kept looking at the valet guy as if that didn't have anything to do with me.

"You love rolling your eyes," he said.

"Your car should be pulling up any second now Ms. Jefferson," the valet guy said.

"Thank you," I replied.

"We're gonna have to break that habit," he said.

"We're not breaking anything," I whispered as I moved to the other side of the booth to wait for my car.

"Do you talk to all your Doms like this?" he asked.

"You're not my Dom and don't say that

160

again," I said.

I saw my car pulling up so I straightened my posture and looked straight.

"Can I ask why you're barefooted and holding your shoes instead of wearing them?" he asked.

I looked down at my fresh manicure standing on the pavement and I rolled my eyes harder.

"Here you are mam," the valet driver said as he held my door open for me to enter.

I got in.

"No good bye?" Malroy asked.

I closed my door.

I could see his black ass standing outside just smiling as I pulled off.

I turned on my phone's Bluetooth and started to call Kara. Then I thought about it. I would be there in 15 minutes and this was one of those moments I needed to lie in the bed, watching our favorite movies, and discussing this theatrical time I've had away. On the drive to Cookie's place I thought about how Kich looked and how much he wanted me to stay with him. I knew I would have to decide sooner or later. I was going to make it later and much later. I was going to make it as late as I could without Kich kidnapping me or without him leaving me. Kich just needed to trust me.

I pulled in the gate and parked my car. I stuck my feet out the car and wiggled them in my shoes. I stood up and headed for the house.

I didn't know if Kara was home or not because she sometimes parked her car in the garage and the door was closed at the moment.

I went to her room and tapped on the door.

"Come innnnn," she said.

"Kara!" I slung the door open and ran in and jumped on top of her.

"Ewww get off of me. Didn't you have that dress on yesterday on your Snapchat?" she joked.

"Umm no, because I didn't even post to my Snapchat yesterday so take that," I said.

"Although I should've because yesterday was amazing," I said.

"Well anyways I need the deets I feel like I haven't talked to you in years. You really went MIA this time," she fussed.

"Kara I don't even know where to start. It's like I was in a different world this entire week and now everything is back to normal and I have this huge pain in my chest," I rolled off of her and onto the bed.

"Why do you have a pain in your chest? Is that in a figurative or literal manner? I'm tryna see if I should call the ambulance," she said.

"Figuratively speaking and it's because I didn't want to leave Kich," I said.

"We had such an amazing time together and I wished I was going back to Memphis with him," I said.

"Then go. What's keeping you here? You and Kich can go anywhere. You're about to blow up with your writings and Kich is already

162

successful. Be a power couple. Be free," she ranted.

"I fucked the valet guy," I blurted out.

"Bitccccchhhh," she said.

"Was it good?" she gave me a reassuring look with the biggest smile and twinkle in her eyes.

"Yes it was good but he's like Kich number two. And let me tell you, I refuse to deal with two of him," I said.

"Well you can sure give him to me," she joked.

"Girl you can have him. He thinks he's going to take me from Kich. He has another thing coming. That will never happen. It was just spontaneous, *he's fine,* sex.

"So what's the problem if you don't want him then how is that interfering with Kich?" she asked.

"Because it's not him that I'm worried about. It's my actions that I'm worried about," I said.

"It's like I get a rush sometimes and I love acting on it. And Kich doesn't mind as of now but what if things change? What if Kich continues to fall for me and now my freedom is gone in every way but I'm stuck living in a house with Melanie and whoever else," I continued.

"Well you should address your fears to him as well. Is it so bad making Kich your only lover?" she asked.

"Well no it's not bad but I know me. If I

have to see him being with someone constantly I'm going to want to do my own thing," I said.

"Y'all relationship confuses me," she said.

"Girl it's just an open relationship I suppose. Kich just doesn't want me to love anyone more than him because he fears that will allow them to take me from him. That's why he's so threatened by my relationship with Zay," I said.

"Situationship," she coughed.

"Ha ha ha. Shut up bitch," I said.

"But seriously that makes sense. Should he be worried?" she asked.

"You know...there's a blessing and a curse in what I have with Zay. The blessing is that logically I see him for all that he is and I no longer want anything to do with that. The curse is once I've truly loved a person an ounce of me always will," I said.

"A lot of times I see it's better for me to not go back and they can never get another chance, but I'm scared. I'm scared of what I would do if he ever acted right. I'm scared that if he did it in time it would change everything and I don't want that. I don't know how to tell Kich that," I said as my eyes started to water.

Kara went to her bathroom and got me some tissue.

"Thanks. I'm ok. I'm ok," I said.

"I'm tired. I'm so tired. I really want to be all the way free. I want to look him in his face and feel nothing," I said.

"You'll get there. It takes time and he was

just in your bed. There is nothing Kich can do within a week to erase all traces of Zay. And although you don't want to admit it. There's not a dumb ass move Zay has done in a week to make you hate him," she said.

And she was right. I hated it. I hated it with everything in me. I hated that it was something in me telling me to let Zay go and something in me still cared.

Gogh

Maybe I'm delusional,
I've lost sight of what love is.
Is it even still possible for you to love me?

I was always in the picture,
so how come I was the one pushed from the frame?

Me.

I'm only guilty of one and that's you.
I think of you daily, this is unhealthy.

But they're good thoughts, it feels wrong.
I try to convince myself that you are bad,
so maybe I'll see all the reasons we aren't meant,
I gotta move on.

165

Silly me, I hear your heart not your talk.
I see your intentions not your actions.
Hear I go again, delusional.

Delusionally in love - that's me.

      I finished catching Kara up with everything that had happened. I even told her about the details during sex with each partner, me and Melanie bonding, Kich asking Rama to come to his party, etc. Every little thing that happened I painted the picture for her so she wouldn't be out of the loop on anything.

      After I was done I went to my room where I stayed the remainder of the day just thinking.

      That's when I wrote that poem in my journal as I recapped on my week.

      Gogh.

      Because I feel crazy like my favorite artist.

      I looked up at my "Starry Night" picture on the wall.

      And then I added a side note prayer.

      Dear God, please remove Zay from my heart. It hurts.

      I was just about to go to sleep when I received a message from Kich.

Kich

Vistoria.

166

Yes.

Promise me.

Promise you what?

That'll you'll never
misread my love
for you.

I don't.

Tell me you won't.
Not now. Not ever.

I won't.

My love for you
captivates every
part of my body
and almost gives
me a feeling I'm
not used to. It's like
you've changed my
will to live. Every
breath I've taken
after I met you
was for you and
because of you.

That's the most
beautiful thing I've

167

ever heard in my life.

I don't use these
words lightly
and I don't use
them for flattery.
I mean every word
I have spoken to you.

I believe you Kich.
You explained that
with so much depth
but I get it. And I'm
grateful to be the
person you love
that much.

I can't wait
to see you.
My birthday party
is in two weeks.
I'll be doing
a lot of planning.
It's going
to be amazing.
I'm going
to send you
money so
you can get
yours, Kara,
and Rama's

plane ticket.

How did you
know Kara
was coming?

She's your
best friend.
I don't have
to be told
that.

Oh right, lol.

You can check
 your account now.
The money
should be there.

Thank you
Daddy.

Well I'm about
to get some sleep.
I just got back to
my home. Ttyl.

I did as I was told and I went immediately
to purchase our tickets. I got Rama's information
so I could get hers. I already knew all of Kara's
info. I called the airline right after to be sure we

had seats next to each other. It just made way for better selfies when you all could sit together on the plane.

All of the days leading up to our departure were mainly a big, boring, blur. Nothing even remotely interesting happened. All I could think about was getting to Kich. Anything that didn't have to do with him was basically a cliff note in my mind.

Kich calling

"Hello."
"How's my baby?"
"I can't do this anymore."
"What's wrong Vistoria?"
"This feels like I'm dying Kich. I just want to be with you."
"Vistoria I've made you an offer but you refused. You didn't have to be away from me for one day but you have to be independent. You have to be free. You need time to get yourself together and decide. I don't like to see you hurting but you can't say I didn't offer you a solution."
"I know, it just hurts so bad. But I'm trying to be strong. I only have a week left. They say absence makes the heart grow fonder. I think I literally feel my heart stretching because it's trying to get to you."
I laughed.
"See a little joke. You're doing better already. How can I cheer you up from here?"

170

"Unless you can make me cum to calm me down I don't see a way."

"I'm about to FaceTime you."

Kich FaceTime calling

I tried to throw my hair in my face to look sexy. I ran to my purse and grabbed a little pink lipstick. I added it to my lips and rubbed them together.

"Hey Daddy."

"What are you wearing?"

"Just my bra and panties."

"Let me see."

I slowly raised the camera and then I scaled my body from my panties to my bra and then to my face so he could get a full look.

"Take your bra off."

I took my bra off.

"I want to see you lick your tits."

"I don't think they will fit in my mouth."

"Try."

I lifted my boobs as close to my mouth as I could get them and then I started to lick on them. I swirled my tongue around and bit on my nipple.

"Just like that. Daddy likes that."

"Take your panties off."

I tried to slide out of my panties while holding it with the other and it wasn't working too well.

I can get my tripod.

"Hold on one second Daddy. I'm going to

171

get my tripod out of the closet so I won't have to keep balancing the phone."

"Hurry, you have Daddy rock hard."

I sat the phone up on my table next to my bed. I then hopped off the bed and opened my two-door closet. I reached to the top of the closet and grabbed my tripod bag. I closed the closet and waved to Kich to let him see I had the bag.

"Daddy is getting impatient."

"Just wait. It'll be worth it."

I took my tripod out of the bag and threw the bag on the floor. I pulled out the three legs and added a little height to each one. I then unscrewed the top of my selfie stick that holds the phone and twisted it into the tripod slot. I picked my phone up and slid it into the base that came from the selfie stick. Then I smiled at Kich and started dancing to show him I was now hands free.

"You had to build an entire skyscraper but I am impressed."

"Thank you."

I said and smiled at the phone.

"Now where were we?"

I sat the phone on the edge of my bed so it was like he was there watching me. I angled the phone on the tripod down so he could see me taking my panties off.

"Yes Daddy likes this view."

I stretched my legs up and slid the panties up then I bent my legs to unwrap the panties from my feet.

"Keep your legs just like that."

172

I kept my legs bent.

"Now straighten them back out."

I straightened my legs back out.

"Now open your legs and spread your pussy for Daddy."

I did as I was told. I was so wet from my FaceTime call with Kich.

"I see my baby is dripping. Pat that pussy for me."

"Spread it. Taste it. Where are your toys?"

Luckily I kept a chest of toys and things right in the corner next to my bed. I pulled out my dildo.

"Get out Daddy's favorites."

Kich had bought me a bound kit full of toys and BDSM restraints.

"Let's see what can Daddy have you use where your hands are still free?"

"I can cuff my feet."

"Did I ask you to speak?"

"No."

"For that let's start with a mouth gag."

I took the mouth gag from my bag and put the ball in my mouth and latched it from the back.

"Good a silent bitch. My favorite."

"Now take out your spreader bars."

Spreader bars were these metal bars that you adjusted around your thighs so they couldn't close. You wrapped a latch around each thigh and the bar made it impossible for you to close your legs.

"Just how I like my sluts."

173

"Now stick your dildo in your pussy."

I didn't know which one and I couldn't talk because my mouth was gagged. I went in my chest and held up different kinds.

"Use the rabbit."

Kich like my dildo that looked like a rabbit because it had two smalls ears that stuck out which were intended to massage the clit while the thicker part was inserted in my vagina.

I managed to get it and stick it in my pussy while my legs were mechanically spread wide open.

"That's a good slut."

"Do you like it?"

"Of course you do. That's what sluts do."

Kich just kept giving his commentary and for a second it felt like he was there.

"Yes you have my dick about to explode."

"Ahh ahhh."

"No don't you cum yet slut."

"You better wait for daddy."

"Hold it."

"I can't."

Those are the words I tried to get out of my mouth through the gag.

I slowed my movements up some so I wouldn't cum yet.

"Ok, Ok. You can cum now. Cum on Daddy's dick."

I could hear in Kich's voice that he was at his peak too.

I increased my speed and motion and then

174

it came. I released all over my dildo, on my bed, with my restraints on, in front of an audience of one.

"That's my dirty whore."
"Pull it out of your pussy slowly for Daddy."

I did as I was told.

"Now you may unlatch your thighs."

I lifted my hands and freed my right thigh and then I freed the left. My legs flopped down. It felt good to close them.

"Now take your gag out and look at Daddy."

I sat up on the bed and took my gag out and smiled at the phone.

"How do you feel?"
"I feel great. Sleepy."
"Well now my baby won't be upset anymore and you can get some sleep."
"Thanks Daddy."
"Go to bed."

I ended our FaceTime call and took my phone from the tripod. I sat the tripod on the floor. I then scooted back up the bed and plugged my phone in the charger and climbed under the cover. That was just what I needed to knock the edge off. I was having a hard time with missing Kich but he was doing a good job at trying to help me fill the gap.

I was happy as the countdown for the final days for me to be with Kich again started. A few days before we left Rama, Kara, and I went shopping for our weekend trip to Memphis. I invited them out so they could get acquainted. I didn't want their first time meeting to be on the airplane. I also wanted to make sure they both were prepared and had some sexy outfits for Kich's party. Kara had an understanding of what to expect but Rama had no idea.

"So you do get this isn't a regular party? And it's mandatory that you have your best fit ready?" I asked Rama.

We decided to all meet at Perimeter Mall because Rama had to meet with someone on that side of town. It was nice to visit that area and they had affordable clothing stores in the mall. I knew we could get some nice things and find a good spot to eat at afterwards. I enjoyed going near Perimeter. It was like it was always shining bright over there and the landscaping was always on point. The flowerbeds always lined the sidewalks so beautifully.

"Yes you've said that over and over without fully giving me the details of the party," Rama said.

"Honestly I can't give you the full details of the party because I don't know them yet. All I know is that there are a lot of eligible bachelors or ladies there depending on how you float and you want to be on your A-game," I said.

"Yes because last year was crazy and I hope it's even more intense this year," Kara ranted.

"Oh gosh I'm so excited. I've never done anything like this before and it's at Kich's house which is even more awesome," Rama said with much excitement.

"We leave in two days," Kara squealed.

"Uhhh I know right. It has been the longest two weeks without Kich," I said.

"But hey you did it and I'm proud of you. I surely thought you were going to row a boat to him on those nights you were drowning your bedroom in tears," she joked.

"Kara that is not even funny," I said.

We all went in this store that sold very sexy attire. It made me feel like all exotic dancers shopped there. We had to get something nice for Kich's party. The requirements were all black but that could be in so many different types of clothing. It could even just be black underwear. As long as it was black.

Rama came with me in the dressing room to see me try on some of my looks. I decided to go with the most risqué one of them all. I got an all lace look that had a black patch over each nipple and that's it. I was going to wear some black lace panties to match.

I also got these super sexy platform heels that were awesome for dancing in because of the bottom. The bottom of the shoe gave me balance. I had danced for Kich in a pair similar to the ones I picked to match my look. I got an all-black pair that where see-through at the top.

"This is practically being naked," Rama said as she saw me trying on my dress.

"I know," I said.

"This doesn't look like anything you would wear to a party where everyone is going to see you. This looks like something you would just wear for Kich in private," Rama said.

"I get it Rama. You don't quite get my attire. But Kich has a very free home. Just know that anything goes," I said.

"I just don't know if I want to wear something like that," she said.

"And you don't have to. My 1st party I believe I wore a long black dress with slits and Kara wore a body suit," I said.

"You're just trying to make me feel better and not feel like a lame," Rama said.

"Look at it this way. You're going to be the sexiest person there anyways because you're going to be performing in aerial silks.

"As a matter of fact, what did Kich tell you to wear for your routine?" I asked.

"I'll be in a black bralette with studs poking out of it and high-waist, fishnet stockings," she said.

"With no panties on?" I laughed.

"Stori," she hit me.

"That's not funny. I don't need to wear panties because the high-waist are made of cloth. It's only the leg part that is fishnet," she said.

"Well shoot, just wear that and call it a day," I said.

"I have to wear something while I'm outside. I can't just wear that around all day," she said.

178

"You're making this more difficult than it has to be," I gasped.

"Sorry," she said.

"No it's ok," I said.

"This is just new to me," she said.

"I tell you what. Just wear a black trench coat over your outfit and that's the look," I said.

"You think so?" she asked.

"Yes, I love it. That's your look and you're not changing. That way you don't even have to change for you performance. You can simply take your coat off and you're ready," I said.

"Ok, I'll do that," she said.

"See now that wasn't hard," I said.

We left out of the dressing room and I called Kara.

Calling Kara

"Where are you?"

"I'm in the store next to you guys. I left out and found some things I liked better over here."

"Well I'm about to pay for my things and then I'll come see what you got."

I hung up the phone and got in line to pay. I didn't like to be on the phone while checking out it always seemed rude to me.

I used my card from Kich to pay for my things and then we went to find Kara.

I walked in the store next door and headed for the fitting room area. I knew that's where Kara would be. As I got closer and closer to the fitting room area I noticed I was in a store that seemed to specialize in fetish clothing. There were chains and whips the closer I got to the back.

"This is my kind of store," I said.

"What kind of things are you guys into?" Rama asked.

"Are you scared?" I asked.

"No, just curious," she said.

"Hmmm....interesting," I said.

"Kara. I'm out here," I called to her from the exit of the fitting room.

She walked around wearing this leather hanging cape with a hood top. It had three latches in the front that barely covered the boobs. Her bottoms were leather panties and thigh-high leather , black boots.

My mouth dropped.

"Bitch I feel some type of way. You're upstaging me like shit and it's my nigga party," I said.

She started laughing.

"I just wanted to channel my inner dominatrix," she said.

"Now I really don't believe I'm ready for this party," Rama said.

"Rama it will be ok. Trust me," I said.

But the truth is I was just trusting Kich. He had saw something in Rama and he believed she was ready. I was just following his orders.

"Stori it's still time if you want to get a feisty look like mine," Kara danced in her outfit.

"It is hot but Kich already said he wanted

me in lace so that's what I got," I said.

"But I believe your look fits you Kara. I can't wait to see it get its debut at the party," I said.

"So Rama what did you decide on?" Kara asked.

"Well Stori thinks...," she started but I could tell she was nervous so I cut in.

"Rama will be wearing her performance look. A studded bralette and fishnet stockings all tucked under a trench coat for the great reveal," I said.

"Nice, I can't wait to see that on your figure," Kara said.

"You're just being nice," Rama said.

"Girl you have a banging figure. There's no lie in that statement," Kara said.

Rama smiled.

"So it looks like this was a successful shopping day," I said.

"I would say so," Rama said.

"Definitely. Well let me go change and pay for this," Kara said.

After Kara came out and paid for her things we went to get something to eat. After that Rama got in her car and Kara and I headed back home. It was a successful girl's trip out. I was on a high and looking forward to seeing Kich. Nothing was going to change my mood or alter that.

Kara and I arrived home and went to our rooms. I was so excited that I took down my suitcase to start packing some of my things. I didn't even want to hang my sexy lace dress up. I put it straight in my suitcase and headed to my closet to pull out everything else I wanted to take. And then my phone went off.

I hope it's Kich so I can tell him what I bought today.

I looked at my phone and it was Malroy. I did not feel like entertaining him. I wished he would just let our moment die out. It was meant to be spontaneous. It wasn't meant to be for life.

Chapter 5
Territory

Malroy

I need to see
you tonight.

All I could do was roll my eyes.

>You don't need
>to see me.

I really do.
I need your
energy. Be my
kitten.

>What you want
>I can't give you.

I just want
you.

>That's my point.
>It will never work
>between us. And I
>love my Dom. I
>don't want to grow
>with a new one.

I don't believe that's
a choice you can

make from one date
and one time
of sex.

                                    The decision I can
                                    make is that I
                                    am in love with
                                    him and there's
                                    no need
                                    in messing
                                    what we
                                    have up for
                                    a potential.

Even someone
who could
potentially be
better for you.
I would choose
after I had given
every alternative
a chance.

                                    It was supposed
                                    to be fun
                                    for the night
                                    and that's it.

He's a polygamist.
He's never going to
choose just you.
So why only

choose him?
I say the more
the merrier.

How is that
your concern?

Because if
you choose
me I would
choose you
back.

I have chosen
and I am ok
with that choice.
I know what
I signed
up for and
I can live
with that.
Before you
try to diss
my Dom
remember it was
because of how
free he is
that allowed
you to even
meet me
and to get
to experience
a taste.

And he is a fool
for that.

No he isn't
a fool he is
confident in his
place. He's ok with
sharing a piece
because he knows
the whole meal
belongs to him.
It may scratch
the surface but
it wasn't intended
to get you full.
So who's the fool?

Wow, so you're
really sticking
up for him?

He wouldn't do
anything less for
me.

Let me prove it
to you.

Prove what?

Let me come
over tonight
and I'll show
you that I can more
of what you need
and desire than him.

I don't think you
get that when I
1st met him
gravity shifted for
me. I've never had
that effect
with anyone.

I believe you didn't
have it with me
because you didn't
allow it. I'm about
to call you I want
to hear your voice.

Malroy Calling

"Stori."
"Yes Malroy."
"You have me pleading for you to give me
a chance and totally stepping outside of my role."
"You can step outside of your role because
at this point you don't have one with me."

"Why are you being so difficult? Didn't we have a good time together?"

"We had a good moment but I'm happy where I'm at. I don't feel the need to leave a place I'm content at."

"Contentment can be dangerous. It weeds out the chance for growth. Don't you want to explore things that he could never unlock for you?"

"You talk a lot of big game but I don't even know what that all means. And honestly I don't know what you could awaken me to that he hasn't already."

"Let me come to you tonight. And show you a piece of my world."

"Ok."

"Ok? So you're going to let me come see you?"

"Yes I don't see what harm it could do. He's out of Atlanta so there's no rule against me seeing someone else I just have to be sure to tell him about it afterwards."

"I'm on my way."

"Well hurry because I have a busy day tomorrow preparing for my flight."

"Your flight? Where are you going?"

"I'm going to Memphis to be with my Dom. It's his birthday and he's having a big party."

"I'm coming just in time to make sure you're thinking about me the entire time you're at that party."

"You're very cocky. I don't know what you

189

plan to do tonight that you didn't the first time
that's supposed to blow me away."
"I'm picking you up and I'm taking you to my
world."
"Is that so?"
"Yes and I'm already in the car so send me
your address."
"Ok, I' m sending it now."
"See you in a little bit Dimples."
"Ok Malroy."
"Ok King..."
"Ok King Malroy."

I decided to take a quick shower before
Malroy came. I didn't know if he was the type to
like showered pussy or scented vagina. He didn't
specify.

Maybe I should call him and ask.

Calling Malroy
Ring
Ring
Ring
Ring
Ring
Ring
"Hey you reached me. You know what to
do when you hear that beep."

*Hmmm...that's weird. I don't know why he
wouldn't answer the phone. Well I'm going to go
ahead and get in the shower.*

I grabbed a silk gown and hurried to the

shower. I didn't know how long it would take him to get to my place because he was already in the car when I gave him my address.

I showered and lotioned my body with one my favorite cucumber body lotion and fragrances. I went and looked at my phone to see if Malroy had called. I didn't have anything. I sat down on my bed and turned on the TV. I figured that would make some time pass by.

Before I knew it I was waking up. I had dosed off and I hadn't even noticed. I grabbed my phone to see if I had any missed calls.

Oh gosh he's probably cussing me out.

I looked at my phone and there was nothing. I looked at the last time I had talked to Malroy and it had been over two hours. I quickly hit call to see what he was doing.

Calling Malroy
Ring
Ring
Ring
Ring
Ring
Ring

  "Hey you reached me. You know what to do when you hear that beep."
What the fuck?
So I called again.
And again.
And again.

191

Calling Malroy
Ring
Ring
Ring
Ring
Ring
Ring

"Hey you reached me. You know what to do when you hear that beep."

Then my breathing increased and my chest started to tighten. He was ditching me.

Was this some kind of sick joke? Is this some attempt to reciprocate how I've made him feel? Very mature. He better not ever dial or think of my number again.

I erased his thread from my phone and deleted all calls associated to his name. I then changed his name to **DO NOT ANSWER**.

I sat there for a moment on the edge of my bed. And I felt it. That feeling of being ashamed of myself. That feeling of wondering what I was doing and why did I care. Why did I care if some guy I just met stood me up? And then it hit me. The trigger. I cared because it hit me like Zay and I was now in a world wind of emotions.

No, you're not. You better not fucking cry. And they wonder why Kich has outrun them all. As fucked up as Kich is he doesn't desert me. Not now. Not ever.

Kich

Daddy.
I love you.
Thank you.

How was your
shopping day?

It was awesome.
You're going to
love what I got.

I'll love anything
my Princess is
in. Get some
sleep.

Ok Daddy.
Night.

Good night
Vistoria.

I lied back down at peace. If no one loved
or respected me Kich did. My twisted, sadistic
lover that I would trade for anyone. And with that
reassurance I went to sleep.

I woke up that morning feeling at peace
and happy I would be seeing Kich tomorrow
morning. My flight left at 6AM the next morning.

I lied in bed and looked up at the ceiling and cherished the sun rays coming through the window. I picked up my phone to text Kich.

Kich

Good morning.

Good morning my love.

I get to
see you soon.
I made it.

Yes you did.
I knew you would.
Better start packing.

Yes Sir.
Ttyl.

I skipped to my closet and proceeded to grab some clothes and shoes. I grabbed enough clothing for my 3 day weekend. I also made sure I grabbed some lingerie as well. I didn't need to pack my toys because I had tons at Kich's place. I heard my phone go off so I picked it up.

DO NOT ANSWER

I am so sorry.

I put my phone back down and proceeded to the bathroom to see what I would need to pack. I heard my phone go off again and I ignored it. Then I heard it ring. I realized there wasn't anything in the bathroom that wouldn't already be at Kich's place so I excited it. I grabbed my extra makeup and put it in my duffle.

I have to remember to get my other makeup from Kich and my new boots.

I had forgot to ask Kich to mail me my items I left in the hotel after he was trying to kidnap me. I guess it wasn't much of a point because I was going to see him in a few weeks. Although I did miss my transparent boots. They were so cute.

I made sure my luggage had my portable phone charger and I closed my bag. Once I was done I had a rolling duffle bag and a matching backpack for my carry-on.

I have a lot of hours to spare. I guess I should find something to occupy my time. I know.

I looked in the mirror.

I'll go get something done to my hair. I've had this same sew-in for a while.

I ignored Malroy's messages and went straight to Kich's.

Kich

Can I cut my hair?

Not too short,
but yes.

Ok :)

I sat an appointment at the salon in *Be Live*.
I heard that the stylist in there were beast at cutting
hair. I decided I wanted to get my hair cut in an
asymmetrical bob.

Rama

You working today?
I'm headed your way
to get a haircut.

Girl no. You know
I'm freaking out
about this party.
I'm getting my
last minute things
together. And be sure
you get Sonja.
She's the best
at cutting hair.

Ok I will.
Thanks boo.
And calm down.
It will all be ok.

196

The party
will be fun.
It's not to
overthink.
It's to enjoy.

I'm going
to try to.

I called the salon back to be sure Sonja was in and she was. I quickly cut the strings of my sew-in. I pulled out my wefts and took my braids down. After that I washed and conditioned my hair. My curly hair was very pretty and I almost didn't want to get it cut.

It's hair. It'll grow back.

After that I put some leave-in conditioner in my hair and put it in a ponytail. I exited the bathroom and went to my closet to find something to put on. I grabbed an over-sized nude sweater with some ripped shorts. I put on some black, thigh-high boots. I then got my keys and purse and left my room.

I want to go ahead and put my luggage in the car since it's packed.

I grabbed my duffle bag and backpack filled with all of my goodies and exited the room.

I stopped by Kara's room before leaving the house.

I knocked on the door.

"Hey, have you seen Cook?" I asked.

"You know she's on vacay with one of her

boos," she said.

"Oh it totally slipped my mind. I feel like I haven't seen her in days," I said.

"Well you would have but you were also gone for days before she left so that's why," Kara said.

"Oh yea, you're right. Well I'm headed to go get my hair cut," I said.

"Oh nice, what are you getting?" she asked.

"I'm getting an asymmetrical bob," I replied.

"That's going to be cute on you. I can't wait to see it," she said.

"What are you doing today?" I asked.

"Girl you know me. Wasting time and packing at the last minute," she laughed.

"As usual. Well let me get to this salon so I'm not there all day," I said.

I left the house and got in my car to head to the salon.

I put my phone on over the Bluetooth to listen to music.

I was speeding down I-75S blasting my music when a call interrupted it. I looked down and it was Malroy.

Why blow me up now? Idiot.

I cleared the call and kept driving.

I made it to *Be Live* and pulled up to the valet area. I gave them my keys and hopped out as fast as I could. I didn't want to see Malroy. I made it into the salon without seeing a familiar soul.

I entered the spa and there was Sarah still

at the desk.

"Hi, I bet you don't remember me," I said.

"Of course I do. You used just about every service we offered your last time here except the salon," she laughed.

"Well I'm here to use that today," I said.

"Of course you are. Do you have an appointment already?" she asked.

"Yes I'm booked with Sonja," I said.

"Ok and you're just in time. I'll have her come up here and meet you now," she said.

I stood there and I picked my phone up to see if I had any messages from Kich. Nothing. Just Malroy.

Maybe you should try to hear him out. He could have an excuse.

Yeah an excuse conveniently mixed with me allowing him to finally come see me and him standing me up.

I erased the thoughts and focused on how happy I was to be seeing Kich again.

"Hey are you Vistoria?" Sonja asked.

"Yes I am," I said.

Sonja was a light to caramel toned, black woman. She appeared to be in her 40's possibly 50's but you know black women age beautifully so it was hard to tell. She had long black hair that silhouetted her face.

"Right this way Ms. Vistoria," she led me to her work area.

"So you're getting a cut today?" she asked as she unraveled my ponytail.

"Yes," I said.

"I got you covered," she said as she wrapped me in a *Be Live* client cape.

I trusted her with my hair because everyone said she was the best.

She straightened my hair before she cut it. I watched as strands of my hair fell on the cape and then onto the floor.

I heard my phone go off again and I pulled my right hand from under the cape to see who it was. It was Malroy ...again. I knew I probably should've answered him but I was tired. I was tired of giving men my attention who treated me like him and Zay. I was fucking tired.

"All done. This cut will even be cute if you wear it with your curly hair," Sonja said.

She spun me around and I looked in the mirror. I loved it. It was very edgy. She still left me plenty of length it's just one side was shorter than the other. I touched my hair and it felt like a feather.

"Yes, I am in love. Thank you so much Sonja," I reached from under my cape and hugged her.

"You're welcome," she said.

I was sure to tip her when I signed the receipt. And since I was there I went ahead and got my nails redone because it was time. I couldn't charge it to Kich's room but that was ok because I charged it to my card from him.

After I paid for my mani and pedi I heard

my phone go off as I was exiting the spa. I figured it was Malroy again, but it was Kich calling.

"And why are you at *Be Live?*"
"And that's not creepy. How do you know where I'm at?"
"You did just use your card that I'm over at that location."
"I'm here getting my hair cut and getting my nails done. I didn't know that was a crime."
"I'm not in the mood for your sarcastic bitch fits right now. You sure you're just not trying to see your little friend again?"
"No I'm not because I don't have to come here to see him and if I was is it a problem seeing him?"
"No it's not a problem as long as he knows his place and you too."
"You know I know my place Kich. You should never worry about that."
"That must be a joke Vistoria. You're spoiled and ungrateful. I don't know if you're going to dip on me again."
"Kich I told you I don't want to keep hearing about that. You definitely weren't an angel in that situation. You left me in the hotel without giving me any explanation. I had to have my best friend come pick me up. I love you but let's not act like we both haven't done fucked up things. I don't throw your shortcomings up in your face although they hurt me and I don't want to keep hearing what I've done either."

"You're right. I just lose my cool when it comes to you."

"I know but you have to get better at that. You have to trust me. Now tell me straight up am I forbidden to see Malroy or not?"

"Malroy is it? And no you're not. If he adds entertainment to your life when I'm not present then I'm ok with that. But..."

"No but...."

"You're right. No but."

"Well I'm heading to pick my car up and then I'm going back home to prepare for my trip. I will talk to you later Sir."

"Yes you will. Enjoy the rest of your day."

If you're done with Malroy why ask Kich for permission? Because you're not done.

Shut up.

Whore.

I headed towards valet and then I saw him. Malroy was at the booth and smiling at me with those pretty white teeth against that dark chocolate, muscular physique.

I walked out and went to the booth and requested my car.

"We have to stop meeting like this," he said.

"Trust me it wasn't planned. I'm just here getting my hair cut," I said.

"I love the hair cut Dimples," he said.

"Thank you," I said.

The valet guy pulled up with my car and

202

opened the door. Malroy got in.

"Get in," he said.

"Can you get out of my car," I said under my breath.

"Don't make a scene out of this. Get in...now," he demanded.

He was giving me that look. That look of command that I couldn't reject so I obeyed. I got in.

"Malroy I don't have time to play games with you," I said.

"I allowed you to talk me into letting you come see me and you totally disrespected me and didn't even show up. And to add insult to injury you didn't even answer your phone to tell me why. You're not forming any bond I would want to have that way. I'm not in the mood to chase a grown man," I argued.

"Stori, if you would've answered any of my calls or texts today you would've known I got arrested last night," he said.

"Arrested for what? What kind of things are you in to?" I asked.

"I got arrested for 'Super Speeding' Stori," he said.

"What's that?"

"If you go 25MPH over the speed limit the officer has the right to arrest you on the spot and he did. I sat the night in jail," he said.

I could feel my guilt coming.

"Well why were you speeding?" I asked.

"I was speeding trying to get to you Stori

damn. Is that so hard to believe?" he asked.

I looked away.

"No," I said.

"Damn you're so stubborn. I don't see why any man wants your ass as a submissive. You don't follow the rules and you make everything complicated. But yet you're so irresistible," he said as he yanked my Jeep in park behind this building. He then gripped my neck and pulled me into him and started eating my face. He was biting and kissing me everywhere.

"Just say you'll be mine," he said.

"I can't say that," I said.

"Tell me," he said.

"I can't," I said.

He put his hands in my sweater and pulled me closer by my bra strap.

He bit my neck and then threw me into my seat. He turned my car back on and sped off.

"Where are we going?" I said.

"You sit back and ride. You're in my world now," he said.

"I have a flight at 6AM so I have to be back to prepare for that," I said.

"I don't care about your flight. Unless you're getting a surgery when you get off that flight it can be pushed back to a later time," he said.

"Uhhh," I gasped as I turned my head and looked out the window.

All the Atlanta lights looked like they were dancing as he sped through traffic. I loved how the skyline of the city looked at night. It looked like a Christmas movie every time. The city sparkled and made its presence of stardom known.

After about 20 minutes we pulled up to this building that had a parking lot full of cars. It was weird because there was no name on it.

"Get out," he said.

"Hell no. I'm not getting out at some weird looking building with no name on it. It doesn't say open or anything," I said.

"Do you trust me?" he asked.

"No I don't," I said sarcastically and rolled my eyes.

"What did I do Stori?" he asked.

"What do you mean?" I asked.

"Why are you such a bitch towards me?" he asked.

"I'm a bitch who doesn't like being stood up and then kidnapped," I rolled my eyes.

"I'm trying to give you the night I would've given you last night," he said.

"By bringing me to this vacant looking building. You may be selling me off for human trafficking," I said.

"You talk like I'm a stranger," he said.

"You are," I said as I whipped my head around at him.

"So you have sex with strangers? You get in the car with strangers? You give strangers your address?" he asked.

"Obviously I have bad taste in men," I said.

He got out the jeep and walked over to my

side. He opened my door.

"Get out," he said.

"No," I said and looked straight ahead.

He reached across me and took my seat belt off. I sniffed his body scent as he leaned across me and I felt my stomach tighten and my walls clench.

I bit my tongue as a reflex.

He stood back up and looked down in the car at me.

"I felt that. You may as well get out," he said.

"You felt what?" I asked.

"I felt your heart rate speed up. Can you stop being stubborn for a moment?" he asked.

I made a face at him and got out the car. He tried to help me.

"I got it," I said.

"Can you behave while we're here and not embarrass me?" he asked.

"I don't even know where I am," I snapped.

"You're not supposed to," he said and placed his hands over my eyes.

"Walk," he said.

"You have got to be kidding me," I said as I started walking.

"Can I get my purse?" I asked.

"No you won't need any of that," he said.

He kicked on the door and I heard it open.

"Code," the person said.

"Trap door," he said.

"Walk," he said.

"Can I get a mask?" he asked whomever

was at the door.

"Keep your eyes closed," he said.

"Sure ok," I said sarcastically.

He took his hands off my eyes and then put the mask on me.

We started back walking but now he was leading and I was following behind him holding his hand.

I heard dance music as we got closer and I could see lights blinking from the corners of my mask. We stopped and he leaned me against what felt like a bar.

"What would you like to drink?" he asked.

"Walk-me-down," I said.

"Ok, I'll respect that," he said.

"Can you get a Walk-me-down for the lady. Strong on that liquor," he laughed.

"Here drink," he said as he placed my hands on my cup.

"If I die tonight all my friends know I went to that salon and then the cameras will show I left with you," I said as I drank.

"Stori, I would never hurt you in the slightest way," he said.

"And another," he said as he put another drink up to my lips.

I could tell that one was straight liquor. He gave me a lime to suck on and then he turned it sideways and sucked on it with me. Our lips were pressed together and we both drank all the juices in the lime.

I smiled.

"There you go. I knew that would loosen you up some. I didn't want you to see where you were until I got that smile," he said as he turned me around from the bar.

He grabbed my hand again and we started back walking and then we stopped. The music was blasting all around us and I wanted to dance.

He finally took my mask off and we were on a dance floor.

"All this to take me to a club?" I asked.

"Big surprise," I said and hit him.

He grabbed me close and started tonguing me down and grinding on me. He picked my leg up and started humping me. We grinded to the beat and then I looked to my left and saw this couple grinding too.

I looked closely and I realized the girl's dress was up and she didn't have panties on. The guy then stuck his penis inside her and she moaned on the dance floor.

"Malroy, they're fucking," I said.

"Look around Stori. They all are," he laughed.

I looked to my right and one guy had his girl lifted in the air fucking her. He was pounding her as she had both legs wrapped around him.

"What the fuck?" I exclaimed as I rested my head on his chest.

"I think I need another drink," I said.

"I'll go get it. You just stay here and keep dancing I want to watch you," he said.

I kept moving to the beat and swaying

208

while watching him.

A girl walked up to me and started dancing with me.

"You come here often?" she asked.

"No," I said.

"You're beautiful," she said.

"Thank you," I said.

Malroy came back with two drinks.

He poured one in the lovely red haired beauty's mouth. Then he poured one in my mouth. We both kept dancing and he pushed our heads together and we tongued on the floor. I rubbed my fingers across her buttery skin. Her tongue was so soft in my mouth and she was an awesome kisser. Her mouth was so sweet.

"Let's go to the next floor," he said.

He grabbed both of our hands and we followed him.

We walked up the stairs and were faced with another door.

It was very dark and then a small window opened. I saw someone look out. He then opened a lower part of the door and slipped a key out.

Malroy took the key and unlocked a closet. He pulled out 3 robes.

Our red haired friend had already started stripping and she folded her dress and put it in the closet along with her shoes. I followed her lead and took my sweater off and put my boots in the closet. I left my underclothes on and put on the robe. Malroy took all of his clothes off and put the robe on.

He then locked the closet back and tapped on the door.

The guy at the door then opened the door and let us in.

Malroy handed him the key upon us entering and he sat them in this glass by the booth he was sitting at. This area was filled with white beds and fluffy hearts everywhere. It was lit yet not too bright. There were white, rectangle shaped couches lining the perimeter of the room. Malroy took us to sit on one.

A couple was in the center of the room giving each other oral. I watched in amazement.

Malroy looked at me and could see I was intrigued. I realized there weren't any clocks anywhere and I didn't know what time it was. I didn't want to miss my flight despite what Malroy said. My entire two weeks had been fantasizing on getting back to Kich.

"What's wrong?" Malroy asked.

"Nothing I said," and smiled at him.

I looked at the red-haired girl next to me. "I'm sorry, I never got your name," I said.

"Elizabeth," she said.

"Elizabeth, nice to meet you. I'm Stori," I said.

"Nice to meet you Stori," she said.

Malroy walked to the center of the room and lied down. He signaled for Elizabeth to come over.

I kept watching. He took his cock out and she started sucking it. Then another girl stood over

210

him and started melting a candle on his chest. Then some other girl came and started putting clothes pins all over Elizabeth's body. I'm talking on her nipples, on her clit, lining her arms, and legs. I kept watching but I could feel myself getting uncomfortable. If Kich was into this he never went this far with me. Malroy kept looking at me and I could tell he was intrigued. I tried to not show how uncomfortable I was. And then it turned up an extra notch. Malroy started fucking Elizabeth. He got on top of her in missionary. And then a guy came behind him and started licking his ass. I bucked my eyes and kept trying to look normal but this was turning into the most X-rated porn I had ever seen.

Ok, he's bisexual. I didn't know that. I do now.

Then the guy switched and started fucking Elizabeth. Then Malroy started fucking the guy in his ass while he was still on top of Elizabeth. And then it happened. Malroy urinated on both of them.

It looked like a ritual and it looked like they were used to it.

Is he marking his territory?

I was kind of frozen in shock by what I just watched and I wanted to get out. Malroy then motioned for me to come over. I stood up and walked towards him.

"If you choose me you have to welcome them. They are both mine and you will be too," he said.

"Now kneel to your King," he said.

I looked him in his eyes and I stepped back.

"Where do you think you're going Stori?" he asked.

"I'm not staying," I said.

"I told you I wouldn't choose you over Kich and I'm not," I said.

"Stori, kneel," he said as he grabbed my shoulder.

"Stop you're hurting me," I said.

I looked down at his two subs and they both looked high and almost passed out.

"You will be mine," he said.

"I'll get a restraining order first," I said and I kneed him in his dick.

"Stupid bitch," he said as he went down the floor.

I ran up and grabbed the key for the closet out of the cup and unlatched the door.

He was still cradling on the floor.

"Stori, I'm going to get you back," he said.

I rushed to the closet and grabbed my clothes and Malroy's jeans so I could get my car keys.

I ran down the steps and got my car keys out of his jeans on my way down. I was still in my robe rushing through the club of fucking guests. I got to the door and tried to unlatch it but I couldn't.

"Let me out! Now!" I yelled.

The guy at the door unlatched it for me and I ran to my car.

I jumped in my car and my hands were shaking trying to crank the car. I saw Malroy come to the door and I got it cranked. I put the car in gear and sped out of the parking lot. I was in tears and terrified.

He knows where I live.

"Dammit, dammit, Stori," I said.

I looked at the time on my car radio and it was 4:30A.M.

Dammit I have to be at the airport at this time. My luggage is already in the trunk so I can make it. I have to call Kara. I know she's cussing me out.

Calling Kara Poo

"Bitch, where the fuck have you been?"

"Kara, it's a long story. Just go ahead and go to the airport and know that I'll meet you there."

"You sound upset. Are you ok? Stori what's up?"

"It's ok. Bad choice in men that's all. I'll catch you up. I'm ok now."

"Stori, are you sure?"

"Yes, I'll see you in like 30 minutes. I'm speeding through the city now trying to get there. But I'm going to make it."

I made it to the airport and parked my car. I realized I still had on my robe and threw on my sweater, shorts, and boots in the parking lot. I then hopped out and grabbed my bags out of the trunk and hurried to the inside.

I was happy that Kich had paid for my TSA pre-check because it saved my life. The time I

213

saved by having that is why I got to sit on that flight with my girls.

Speaking of Kich. I had 1000 missed calls and text from him. I was scared to even tell him what happened because he may try to kill Malroy.

"You have some explaining to do," Kara said.

"I am so pissed at you. You had me stressed the fuck out. You went MIA for hours," she said.

"I'm sorry. I'm so sorry," I said.

"Well I'm just happy you're here now," Rama said.

"Thanks," I squeezed her hand and smiled.

"I love you guys," I said.

"We love you too," they said and we all hugged.

At that moment I knew that I had to make better choices. Kich may could do the polygamist life but I don't think I could do the polyandry life because I chose men horribly.

I lied my head on Kara's shoulder and I went to sleep. I was so exhausted.

Chapter 6
<u>Nostalgia</u>

"We're here Stori. Wake up," Kara nudged me.

I lifted my head and wiped the slob from her shoulder.

"Sorry," I said.

"Yea, yea," it's not like I'm not used to it.

"I'm sure I stink. I'm glad we're going to the hotel before I see Kich," I said.

"Uhh huh, I can't wait for you to tell me where the hell you were last night," Kara fussed.

"I was there against my will and Kich is probably still screaming at me," I said.

"Oh no Kich. I never responded to him he probably thinks I missed my flight," I said.

I grabbed my phone but it was dead.

"Crap," I said.

"This trip is already starting off crazy," I said.

We took our bags from the overhead bins and waited in line to exit the plane. I could feel my ear popping from the pressure of the plane so I took some gum from my purse to help.

"You guys want some gum?" I asked Rama and Kara.

"Sure," Rama said.

"Yes," Kara responded.

We finally made it off the plane and since it was only a weekend trip none of us had any baggage to claim.

"I have to get to a charger or Kich is going to kill me when he sees me," I said.

I could tell we were near the area where

family waited because people started running pass and hugging their loved ones. I always got a little teary eyed when I saw someone in uniform reuniting with their family. It was something so beautiful and admirable about a person who's been away serving the country and being blessed to make it back. I always appreciated it and I had a gratitude of happiness for that person and his or her family.

As we got closer I saw Rico standing out.

"Oh Kich, must've sent Rico to pick us up. I was just going to call an Uber," I said.

And as the people cleared more I noticed it was Kich and Rico.

I swallowed really hard and tried to fix my hair. I hadn't saw a mirror in hours.

"Oh shit Stori. You're in trouble," Kara laughed.

"No shit Sherlock," I griped.

"Hello Ladies. I'm Rico and I will be driving you to your hotel this morning," Rico said.

Although we could've stayed at Kich's we both agreed on me having a hotel for privacy. In addition, all of his exclusive guest could have the house. We would more than likely stay at the house the night of the party because everyone would be too lit to leave.

"This way Ladies," Rico motioned for us to follow him.

"Not you," Kich stuck his hand out.

He turned and walked away and I followed.

"I'll see you guys later," I said to Kara and

Rama.

"Bye Stori," Rama said.

"Ha ha ha ha," Kara laughed.

I rolled my eyes at her and lifted my eyebrows at her.

I followed Kich out of the airport and his BMW i8 coupe was out front.

"It feels good today," I said trying to lighten the mood.

He said nothing.

He opened the car doors and I got in.

He sped off and I could tell we were headed to his house.

"Are you excited about your party?" I asked.

He said nothing.

We rode a good bit in dead silence.

"Where's your phone?" he asked.

"Kich I can explain. It wasn't my...," I started then he cut me off.

"Where's your phone?" he asked again.

I took the dead phone out of my purse.

"Let me see it," he said.

I put it in his hand.

He looked at it then he rolled the window down and threw it out the window.

"Kich!" I screamed.

"You don't seem to use it. So I figured you wouldn't mind," he said.

I sat back and looked out the window.

I don't care. I have Apple Care anyways and if I didn't he would be paying for it.

I made faces and mumbled to myself while looking out the window.

We made it to his house and nostalgia came hitting me.

Nostalgia II

Back shots.
Back shocks.
Tell me if these words mean anything to
you.
Cattle prod.
Spreader bars.
Armbinders.
Dungeon Irons.
Nostalgia, nostalgia, nostalgia.
Remember me?
The memory.
You feel it; you can smell it.
Wake up, wake up, wake up.
Your coffee in the AM.
8 o' clock, you rise.
3 o' clock, you call.
Come to me, come with me, come.
Nostalgia, nostalgia, nostalgia.
Yes fish, no sushi.
A beating, but no bruising.
Blue dragons, scales, eagles.
Crown, royal, regal.
Dark house, red lights.
Teeth marks, no bites.
Nostalgia, nostalgia, nostalgia.

I got out of the car and headed in the house behind Kich.

He better not hit me or he'll be getting the same thing Malroy got.

As I entered the house Melanie was headed up the stairs.

"Hey Mel," I said.

"Sit," Kich said.

I sat down and looked around.

Kich's house always made me happy. It was something about seeing the fruits of someone's labor that was inspiring.

"I'm interested on how you're sitting there smiling after you've had me sickly worried about you all night," he said.

"It was Malroy," I tried to get it out quickly because I knew if he heard a man's name he would give me time to explain.

"That nigga," he said.

"After I got my hair cut he told me to get in the car with him," I said.

"And where did he take you?" Kich asked.

"Did you fuck him?" he looked at me.

"No, he took me to a club," I said.

"Figures, because he's unoriginal," Kich laughed.

"It wasn't a regular club," I said.

"Trust me, I know what club it was," he laughed.

"It all makes sense now," he said.

220

"I thought that was him," Kich laughed.

"It's a reason I don't take you to certain places. My little baby thinks she's all grown up now," Kich continued.

"Am I missing the joke? I literally ran out of the club because he tried to piss on me," I said.

"It's how he marks his territory. I think it's kind of creative," he said.

"You know I knew I had seen him before at the hotel that day when I caught him locking eyes with you. It all makes sense now that's why it's funny," he said.

"Well you wouldn't think it was funny if he had peed on me. As a matter of fact how do you know he didn't?" I asked.

"Because you're here. If he had marked you he wouldn't have let you come back to me," Kich said.

"So you know Malroy?" I asked.

"We've crossed paths a few times. I mean hey we're both well paid Doms. We can get into the same events," Kich said.

"Oh right. He knows where I live and I kneed him before I left him at the club," I said.

"The crazy bastard probably enjoyed it," Kich laughed.

"Kich I'm serious. I don't want to be afraid to go home," I said.

"Trust me, he won't bother you. But I'll contact some people to be sure he gets the message loud and clear if it will make you feel better," he reassured me.

221

"Yes it will," I said.

"Well, now that I feel better you can go bath and speak to Melanie now," he said.

"Ok," I grabbed my bag and headed upstairs.

I passed by Melanie's room and then I stepped back to knock on the door.

"Hey...Mel?" I turned the knob and peeked in.

"Hey Stori," she smiled. Her room was huge. She was across the room doing yoga.

"I need to be joining you," I said.

"Well come on," she said excitedly.

She went to her walk-in closet and grabbed another mat.

"I love having a girlfriend over to do things with me," she said as she laid the mat down.

"Well I really needed to go shower," I said.

"It's fine you can shower once you're finished stretching with me," she said as she started taking my sweater off.

"Now just take these shorts off," she started to undo my button.

"I got it Melanie. Thanks," I said.

I took my bottoms off and got on my mat she put out for me.

We started stretching while sitting and touching our toes.

"Uhh I use to be able to make my forehead touch the ground while doing this," I said.

"I can help," Melanie said.

She came and sat on my back while I was

stretching forward and touching my toes.

"Oh crap Mel, this hurts. Get up, get up," I said.

"Nope you have to feel it. I haven't got to 30 seconds yet," she said.

At that moment Kich walked in.

"Melanie, what are you doing to Stori?" he asked.

"I'm helping her stretch Papi," Melanie said.

"Stori are you ok?" he asked.

"Yes," I groaned.

"Is it time to let me up yet?" I continued.

"Oh it has been 30 seconds. Yes," Melanie said as she hopped off my back.

"Great to see my family is getting along," Kich said.

"Yeah Melanie is trying to show me how to be as flexible as her," I said.

"Well I'll let you girls get back to stretching," Kich said.

"Bye Daddy," I said.

Melanie and I did some more yoga and then I went to shower in my room. I had a room at Kich's house but I never really used it because I was always with him. I just used it for moments like today when we were not on the best terms and I didn't want to crowd him.

I wrapped my hair up with a satin scarf and then put a shower cap on it so my cut wouldn't get wet and poof up. After I got out the shower I wrapped myself up in my towel and headed back

223

in the bedroom.

I sat on my bed and noticed a bag on the edge of the bed with a pink bow on it.

I opened it and it was a new phone.

How did he get this that fast?

Rico.

I turned the phone on and put in my Apple I.D. and a lot of my information came back. I didn't really care if I had the pictures and things because I needed to clean out the 2,000 photos I had anyways.

I text Kara.

Kara Poo <3

Kich broke my phone.
I have a new one.

And a new number lol.

I'm not surprised.
After dealing with
Malroy a new number
is a good thing.

Yea I didn't
get those
details.

Girl this is way too
juicy you have to call.

***Kara Poo Calling ***

I gave Kara all the tea while I continued to get dressed. I put on a black, crop top shirt. It was cut out in the chest area and the fabric went around my neck like a choker. I paired it with some high-waist leggings and my black thigh-high boots.

I did my makeup and straightened my hair some. Once I was all dressed I got my phone and put it in my purse. I then exited the room to go find Kich.

I walked the halls looking in each door as I passed. Kich's room was near the Power Room.

I stopped by Kich's door but then it caught my eyes as it always had. The Power Room just called me. I kept walking and I wrapped my hands around the medieval door knob and twisted.

I looked inside and there it was in all its glory. It was just like I had always remembered. The one light that always shown down on the circular bed in the center.

"You still sneaking in here," Kich said.

I turned around and smiled.

"Thanks for my phone," I said.

"A new number tho? Is it on your account?" I asked.

"It is, but I did that so Rico could go ahead and get it but you can switch everything over when you get a chance or you can leave it as it is," he said.

"Well thank you. I appreciate it," I said.

"What are you about to do?" he asked.

"I'm about to go catch up with my girls. Do

some eating and some shopping," I said.

"Ok, I'll have Rico pull the truck around," Kich said and he kissed me on my forehead.

I titled my head and gave him a Smurf kiss by rubbing my nose against his.

"I'll see you later," I said and hugged him.

"I hope you're ready for your big birthday bash tomorrow," I said.

"I'm always ready," he said as he poked my arm to make me look down and then he popped my face.

"See it's you who needs to catch up," he joked.

"Ha ha, you're so funny. So where will Rama be performing?" I asked.

"In the Power Room. They'll be setting her equipment up in a little bit. It's going to be exciting," he said.

"You're having her to perform in there. Kich," I said as I hit him.

"People will be having orgies and everything else in there," I said.

"Stori, you worry too much," he turned me around and walked me downstairs.

"Now how do you think I knew what to buy for Rama? She told me and don't you think I told her the extent of what to expect in some form?" he asked.

"Well I don't know. Did you?" I asked.

"Yes I did and she was fine with it," he said.

"Your friends are fine and they can make

their own choices. Let them enjoy this weekend and don't babysit them. They're totally safe so just relax. From what I hear they're both looking forward to the party," he said.

"Ok, you're right," I said.

"Now Rico has been waiting so let's go," Kich opened the front door and walked me to the truck.

"Take care of my prized possession Rico," Kich said as he closed my door.

He tapped the back of the trunk once I was in signaling to Rico he could leave.

I sent a group text to Rama and Kara.

Rama, Kara Poo <3

Headed your way!
It's time to shop and eat.
And eat and eat.
I've missed Memphis
food.

Rama

I'm ready!
Woohoo

Kara Poo <3

It's about time
bitch! I'm hungry!

Lol, shut up
tramp!

Rico pulled into the parking garage of the Peabody and I got out and walked to the hotel room I was supposed to be in before Kich snatched me up.

I walked through the historical hotel admiring the décor. I went to our room and used the key Rico had given me to get in.

"Ladies," I said as I walked in.

"Yay!! You're back," Rama came and gave me a hug.

"You're back with no black eyes. Thank god. I didn't want to have to fuck Kich up," Kara said.

I started laughing.

"Let's go ladies. You know I'm dying to get some Pearl's. Do not play with it," I did an old school bounce dance.

We exited the hotel and headed to the street. I looked at all the businesses I passed on my way to Pearl's Oyster House. Texas De Brazil, Lansky's, Huey's, Blue's City Cafe, BB King's, Flying Fish.

I exhaled.

It always felt good to just be in Memphis.

We finally made it to Pearl's. We walked through the front door and headed to the register so we could be seated.

"How many?" the hostess asked.

228

"Three," Kara said.

"Ok I can get you seated right over here," she said and she walked us to our table.

"Your server will be with you in a minute," she said.

We sat down at our table.

"I don't like how this tablecloth is always on my legs," Kara said as she tried to shift it.

Kara was always being over-dramatic about tables and menus at restaurants.

Our waitress came to the table and was about to give us menus but I intervened.

"We both know what we want you can just give it to her," I pointed to Rama.

"Yes because I don't want that menu near me," Kara said.

"What's wrong with the menu?" Rama asked.

"Nothing," she's just got a menu phobia.

I had grown used to Kara and her menu chronicles. Most times we already knew what we wanted so she didn't have to see it. If she didn't do that then she looked off my menu, used a napkin to flip it, or she would pull the menu up online. It was always funny to laugh at other people's response to her.

"Rama it's really no point in looking because I'm telling you the best thing is the Chargrilled Oysters. Anything else is just second best," I said.

The waitress came back and Kara ordered.

"I'll get half of my oysters raw and the

other half can be Chargrilled," Rama said.

"Ok, you think you gone want them raw ones, but after you taste those Chargrilled you gone wish you had got a dozen of those and not half," Kara said.

"Yeah she's not lying Rama. The Chargrilled Oysters ain't come to play with you hoes," I laughed.

"So what will it be?" our dark-haired, tatted waitress asked. She had that black hair that you could tell she had just put over blonde because the blonde was still peeking through. She had a hummingbird tattoo on her arm that was super bomb. I loved how vivid the colors were in it.

"I'm going to go with half and half," Rama said.

Our orders started to come out. Rama tasted one of Kara's oysters because hers came out 1st.

"OMG, these are delicious," Rama said.

"Told you girl," Kara said as she scooped an oyster out and put it on a cracker.

Rama's oysters came out and we all got one of her raw oysters.

"You have to sprinkle it with some lemon juice. It's so good," I said.

"I like mine with hot sauce," Rama said.

"Ok, I see ya Rama. I didn't know you were a 'hot sauce' in your bag type girl," Kara joked.

We all got our raw oyster and sucked it down at the same time.

"Whoo, I loved how that went down. Like I

felt something explode inside me. I see why they say this is an aphrodisiac," I said as I swayed side-to-side sexually.

"Emmmm," I licked my lips.

"Ok no more oysters for her," Kara said.

"I wish I had eaten this while Kich was near," I said.

"I'm going to have to bring him here," I continued.

"See my oysters made a statement too," Rama joked.

"You're right. They did," I said.

I made sure I posted our outing to all of my social media. We were cute, having fun, and enjoying my favorite city.

"I need like 3 Amaretto sours," I said.

I made sure I told the waitress when she came back to our table. Kara and Rama ordered drinks too.

I posted us downing our drinks too.

We ate and drank good at Pearl's Oyster House.

"That's all I needed," I said.

"What's next?" Rama asked.

"I'm ready to get lit," Kara said.

"Fuck it!! Let's go to 152," I said.

So we paid for our meal and headed over to Club 152 to end our night. I used my Kich card to pay for us a VIP section. It came with complimentary bottles and of course I got the Goose.

I loved 152 because you could always hear

a mix of music. It was a nice looking, very built white guy in the section next to us. He had his friend and his assistant with him. I went over and sat in his lap.

"You like caramel baby?" I asked.

"I love it," he said and passed me a drink.

"What's this?" I asked.

"Fireball," he said.

"Ok, cool," I said and I started to drink.

We then started making out on the couch and he was all in my shirt.

"What is it with white men and boobs?" I asked.

"We love them," he said as he kept bouncing mine.

I felt my phone vibrate in my purse so I took it out. I figured it was Kich because my friends were with me so it wasn't them and no one else had my number.

Kich

I miss my baby.
I don't like you
being in my city
and I'm not seeing you.
You're coming back
here tonight.

daddy im
tryna have fut

232

Fuck, I can barely text right now.

I was about to put my phone back in my purse and I saw my Instagram notifications go off. I checked to see what it was. Zay had commented on one of my pictures. I felt my stomach tie in knots.

What could he possibly want with me?

Chapter 7
<u>Curious</u>

He had commented on an old picture. I scrolled to the bottom to see what it said. I know I probably should've just ignored it but I couldn't. I was curious.

zayphillips

Text me Stori.

I knew his number by heart so I typed it in my messages and hit sent.

+1 (901) 000-7684

It's Stori.

I had to use all my brain power to not look like an idiot.

You in Memphis
ain't it?

Yea.

I wanna see you
can we meet up.

Kich

I don't know what that
was supposed to say
but I'm tryna see you.

Didn't you just

235

say that?

*Wait, are Kich and Zay both texting me.
Did they plan this?*

I was always paranoid when I was under the influence.

"I'll be right back baby," I said to my new body builder friend.

"Kara, Kara, come here," I said.

"Whoooo!! Turn up! Turn up!" Kara yelled as she smacked two Asian girls ass as they twerked.

"Kara, come here," I said.

She walked over.

"Those Asian bitches kissed me," she said.

"Look at my phone," I pushed my phone in her face.

"It's too close up Stori I can't see," she moved the phone back.

"Ok, what about it?" she asked.

"Kich and Zay are both texting me," I said.

"Ok well ignore Zay and let's get back to partying," she said.

"I haven't talked to him since he did that thing to me. I'm gonna bring it up," I said.

"Well bring it up Stori. You didn't need my approval to text him back," she said.

"Yea you're right," I said.

+1 (901) 000-7684

You're a mean person.
Y did you do that
to me?

I'm sorry. I'll
make it up to you.

>You hurt me.
>You always hurt me.

Can I just see you?
I really want to see
you.

>I'd do anything for
>you. I love you.
>I always have.

You crazy Stori.
I hear you.

>I'm not crazy.
>I would've never
>done anything Zay
>if you had just acted
>right. Why won't you
>act right? What did I
>do to make you be
>this way?

I'm just tryna have
fun and you always

tryna be serious.
That's all it was
for me.

I sat down on the white VIP couch
and stared into space. I felt like I had
walked into the twilight zone.

*Why did I always let him do this to
me?*

+1 (901) 000-7684

I wish you would've
told me that from the
beginning.

Don't go getting
in your feelings.

Just tell me
you never cared
and I'll leave
you alone forever.

Nvm, Stori.

Tell me!

Zay!

I sat there quiet by myself.
That's all it was for me.
I know I had said I wouldn't cry over him

again, but I lied. Because I cried. Right there in the club with my friends. Surrounded by everyone living and enjoying life. I cried.

Kara came over.

"Are you crying?" she asked.

"What the hell is wrong with you?" she asked.

"Did that white guy hurt you?" she spun around and looked at him.

"No Kara," I said.

"Well then what is it?" she asked then she picked up my phone.

"Who was the last person you text?" she asked.

"Zay," I said in between my tears.

"See I'm tired of his ass," she said.

"What are you about to do? Give me my phone back," I said.

"You can take it because I'm about to message him from my Facebook," she said.

I saw her fingers typing really fast.

"And sent," she said.

"What did you send? Let me see?" I grabbed her phone and opened her Facebook app.

Kara Smith

Look, I don't know where your head is or what your place is in your life, but I need you to stop coming in and out of my friend's life. How you gone come to our place and then disappear? Then when you KNOW she in Memphis, contact her for your selfish pleasures? She ain't a toy. She may have made some mistakes, but she cares about you and I don't appreciate you dipping in and out of her life hurting her. Find someone else to play with. I don't have time to keep wiping her tears because of a fuck boy who is in denial about what he wants. You don't have to respond, but stay the fuck away from her if you ain't serious. She broke a 3 YEAR celibacy for you. Regardless of what your view of her may be, she doesn't deserve this. Leave her alone if you're not serious.

"Thanks Kara," I said.

"You know I got your back. Always," she said and she hugged me.

"Now let's enjoy the rest of this party," she said.

And that's what we did. We enjoyed the rest of our night and went home. This time in Memphis we didn't have to watch the tourist throwing up in the road because we were the tourists throwing up in the road.

"Kara hold my hair," I said as I vomited on the side of the nightclub, Purple Haze.

I called Kich because at this point I could barely text.

Calling Kich

"I don't think I'm going to make it. I'm so drunk."

"It's ok baby. You can stay there tonight.

I'll see you tomorrow."
"Night."
"Good night Vistoria."

We woke up the next morning and thankfully without hangovers.

"Today is the day," Rama said as she headed to the shower.

"Why are you up and so perky?" Kara asked.

"Because I have to head to Kich's house to practice," she said.

"Oh yea that is today," Kara said.

"Of course, it's today. The whole reason we are here is to celebrate my babe's birthday," I gloated.

Rama left before us because she had to rehearse and be sure all of her performance would be right.

Kara and I lounged around the hotel most of the day and ordered room service. It was one of the perks of staying at one of the best hotels in Memphis. After that Kara got her things for the party and we caught an Uber to Kich's house. My things were there too so we decided to just both change there.

We got there and the yard was already filled with cars.

"Gosh I didn't know this many people would be here this early," I said.

"Me neither and we aren't dressed," she said.

"It's cool. I'm sure we can slip passed them without being seen," I said.

And we did. No one was in the living room area when we slipped in and ran up the stairs. They might've all been in the Power Room. We made it to my room and we both showered.

It's like Kich could smell me because he came to my door a little after we had arrived.

"I see you crept in," he said.

"Yes I did," I said.

I had put my lace dress on now with my show girl heels. I walked over and kissed him.

"You look good," he said and he popped me on my butt.

Kara walked out in her dominatrix suit.

"You're killing that leather outfit mam," I said.

"I say that look becomes you Kara," Kich said and winked.

"I need to go over my hair some more and then I'll be ready," I said.

I put on a masquerade mask and headed to join the party guests.

I knew it was no point in keeping up with Kara because she loved to do her own thing at Kich's events.

I went to the bar to get me a drink and I ran into Ralph.

"What's up Stori," he said.

"Ralph? What are you doing here?" I asked.

"I take it I was invited just like you," he

took his shot and banged the glass back down on the bar.

"You're not usually invited that's why it's odd," I said.

I wonder did Kich invite Zay too.

"Where's the others?" I asked.

"Others?" he repeated me.

"Yea, you have a lot of friends. Where are they?" I asked.

"They didn't come or either they weren't invited," he said.

"Oh...ok," I said relieved.

"They don't really get into this type of thing," he said.

I swayed a little as the Jazz music played and I watched the guest mingling and dancing throughout the house. The chandeliers shined bright but the house still had a dim look to it.

"Oh yea that's understandable," I said.

"Yep...don't worry Zay isn't here," he laughed.

"What's your problem?" I asked.

"I don't have a problem Stori," he said.

"No you do. Did I do something to you? Why is my private life any of your business?" I asked.

"Nothing lil' mama," he said and took another shot.

"If you weren't such an asshole I would hook you up with one of my friends but nope," I said and drank my shot. I sucked on my lime to help the taste.

243

"You good with that mouth," he said.

"Excuse you," I said.

"And I don't want your friend's Stori," he said as he took his last shot and then walked off.

I don't want your friends? Does he want me? He annoys me. He's the reason Zay is mad at me. Fucking snitch.

No you're the reason Zay is mad at you. You fucked Kich on your own. Ralph just told it.

Well he didn't have to tell. It wasn't his business to tell. I bet if I fucked him he wouldn't tell that shit.

Thinking what I'm thinking?

I went to go find Kich to inform him of my plan. I wanted to get Ralph back. I wanted to treat him like the bitch he was. I wanted him to witness firsthand the power I held. I wanted to break him. I was going to break him by giving him exactly what he wanted.

I found him off in one of the rooms with some masked girl with no clothes on.

I walked in.

"Out," I said to the girl.

Ralph stood up and was about to exit too.

"Not you," I said.

"You sit," I said.

I turned on a side lamp. All of Kich's lamps had red light bulbs. It was enough light to see in the dark but not enough to lighten the entire room. It really helped to set the mood that he was so fond of. Sex and more sex.

"So why did you do it Ralph?" I looked

244

him in his eyes with my eyebrows raised and my mouth tight.

"I felt like you were being slick and playing games with my niggas. That shit ain't cool," he replied.

"So you told Zay I was fucking Kich to protect him?" I asked.

"Yeah, pretty much. Bitches like you always tryna come between the bruhs," he said.

"Bitches like me huh?" I repeated.

"That's funny Ralph," I said.

"What's funny?" he asked.

"This whole facade you have going," I laughed.

"I don't know what you talkin' about," he said.

I walked closer to him.

"Stop," I placed my finger on his lips.

"It's apparent what you really want. It's what you've always wanted. You've wanted it since you met me and you can't understand why you've watched others get it and not you," I continued.

"Get on your knees," I whispered in his ear as a nibbled on it.

He slowly got on his knees in front of me without saying a word.

I lifted my lace dress and propped my leg up on a nearby chair.

"Smell it," I said.

Then I grabbed his face and shoved his nose into my lace panties. He grabbed my thighs and started massaging my ass.

"Did I tell you to touch me?" I lifted his face up to look at me.

"No," he replied.

"Well don't. Do as you're told or you won't even get to taste this pussy," I said.

"Ok," he replied.

"Ok isn't good enough for me. When I give you an order I want you to say 'Yes Mistress'. Got it?" I commanded.

"Yes Mistress," he said.

"Good boy," I replied and shoved his nose back into my underwear.

This time my panties had shifted some and my clit was slightly exposed.

"Suck on my clit," I said.

Ralph's lips were really full and wrapped around my clit very tightly. I moaned out in ecstasy.

"Keep sucking it," I continued.

I could hear his mouth popping and slurping on clit.

Bitch what about Tierra?

Fuck Tierra. She's heard my issues with Zay and it didn't stop her from fucking him. She sat in my face, doing my hair, pretending to be concerned all while she wanted him. I'm giving her the details for her to go try her luck. Fuck that bitch. I'm glad her nigga is tasting my pussy. Payback is a bitch and I'm killing all these birds with one stone.

"Is this what you wanted?" I yanked his head back and looked in his eyes.

"Yes Mistress," he replied.

"So are you going to tell this?" I asked.

"No Mistress," he said.

"Oh you don't want to tell how you're enjoying every moment of licking this bitch's pussy huh?" I asked.

"No Mistress," he replied.

"Bite it," I said.

He bit my clit and my shoulders jerked from the intensity.

"That's fine. I can have a lot of fun with you like this," I said.

I readjusted my leg so he could get a better angle inside my pussy.

"Move my panties to the side and lick all of my juices. I want my pussy to be dry when you're done because you've sucked it all out," I said.

"Yes Mistress," he said.

"Good boy," I said.

I used the chair and his face to keep me balanced. My juices covered his nose and mouth completely.

"Do you want to fuck me Ralph?" I asked.

"Yes please," he said.

"Oh fuck I'm cumming," I said as I felt the balloon in my stomach get full and then burst. I pushed his face firmly into my pussy not caring if he had air to breath.

As my shakes slowed I wiggled his face side to side in my vagina.

"Oh yes Ralph. You made my pussy feel amazing," I looked at him and kissed him on his lips.

I then pushed his head back and lowered my leg from the chair.

"Thanks for that," I began to exit the room.

"Guess I'll get back to the party," I said.

He got up from the floor.

"Stori, that's it?" he asked.

"You're not going to let me feel you?" he asked as he pulled me closer into his pelvic area and thrusted against me.

"You haven't earned it," I said.

"Show me you deserve to enter this pussy and then maybe you will," I said.

"You can't just leave man," he said.

"I'm gonna fuckin' go crazy. My dick is swollen like never before," he continued.

"Well I can go get the girl you were about to start on," I said.

"I don't want her. My dick wants you," he said.

"I have to get back before Kich starts looking for me," I said.

Which was a lie. I told Kich exactly what I was going to do.

"Just let me have you," he said.

"Well what are you gonna do about it?" I asked.

See I can spot a bitch nigga anywhere. Kich would've been done flipped my ass and fucked me raw for even thinking I could talk this much shit. But Ralph just didn't have it in him.

"Exactly. We'll continue when I'm ready," I said.

He looked so disappointed.

"I tell you what, since you did such a good job of letting me splash all over your face I'll at least massage your dick while you cum," I bargained.

"Now go sit," I pushed him down on the couch.

What would Zay think if he walked in and saw this?

Who cares bitch. *"It was only fun"* remember?

I got on my knees and started to fondle him. I stroked his pants with my hands. When I got to his dick I pressed it firmly to feel how hard it had gotten. I then began to undo his pants. First, I took the metal button and slid it through the jean hole. Next, I slowly unzipped his pants. I folded back the corners on each side of his jeans and reached in his underwear. I then pulled his cock out and into my hands.

I got really close and then I spit on it.

"Go ahead, play with it. Play with it like you would've done if I left," I said.

What Ralph didn't know is I wanted to put his cock in my mouth so bad. I loved giving head so much it was hard to see a good one in my face and not taste it. I wanted to slide him inside me and buss all over it. However, I didn't because the objective wasn't to give him what he wanted but to

249

show him that I could own him.

He started to stroke it and I cuffed my hands under his balls. His strokes became faster and faster. I spit on it again to excite him.

"I want you so bad Stori," he said.

"I know you do and you will in time," I said.

I continued to help him stroke until he bust everywhere.

"Better?" I asked.

"Yes," he said.

He forgot the "Mistress" but I figured I had put him through enough laboring for one day.

I stood up and exited the room. The little slut I had sent out of the room was still waiting by the door. Kich must've assigned her to Ralph for the night so he wouldn't be totally bored.

"You can go finish him," I said.

I laughed.

These niggas will learn not to play with me. I will break them and own them. Girls really run the world. We are the creators of life. Men are nothing without us and we rule them with our vagina. It can literally give life and take it.

I went and peeked in the Power Room to see how Rama was doing. She was so sexy up there sitting in her yoga hammock while the people under her had riveting sex.

I guess Rama was more into this life than I thought.

I looked closely and she had started playing

250

with herself sitting in her hammock above the crowd.

Kich sensed it.

I got tired of watching everyone have sex so I went to find Kich. I walked downstairs and Kara was on the couch getting head from one guy while another one had his cock in her mouth.

Aren't those the same two men I pulled her away from last year?

It was like everything had become full circle. This was my life. Freaky and kinky.

But are you happy?

I got tired of my inner self always speaking to me and analyzing me. I found Kich in the kitchen and we fucked right there. I was leaking from the head Ralph had just given me.

I slid my panties to the side and Kich stuck his cock in me. He lifted one of my legs in the air and I leaned on the counter while he thrusted upwards in me.

"I love it," I said.

Kich wrapped his hands around my mouth and kept fucking me. Then he released his load inside me.

"Yes Daddy. No one does me like you," I said.

He took it out of me.

"Come clean this dick off," he said.

I got on my knees and licked all of his and my juices off his cock.

"You make me the happiest man alive Vistoria," Kich said.

"Is that true?" I asked as I continued to suck on him.

"Yes," he said.

"What is it that makes you so happy?" I looked up at Kich.

"Obedience," he said as he watched me continue to lick him clean.

"I'm going to move in with you Daddy," I said.

"This has been the best birthday ever," he said.

I smiled at him. The night was amazing. The party was successful. A successful fuckfest. Which in Kich's world is a perfect day. Everyone got pleasured and that was always Kich's goal. I now saw how Kich stayed rich. People paid good money for invites to Kich's parties.

Kich and I went to join the others in the Power Room. We watched as they had sex over and over again. And then they would switch.

Kich dosed off before me so I slipped to my room to get my phone.

I checked to see if I had any messages or missed calls.

Of course you don't genius. New number remember?

I went to my social media to check my notifications. My social media was always blowing up. When I got to Instagram I got a chill thinking about Zay's comment. I didn't even want to think about him or see his comment so I left Instagram. I didn't need his presence to blow my buzz. I went to Facebook instead. I had an inbox so I checked it. It was Lamont. My heart stopped and I felt like I was about to shit in my pants.

Let's rewind to the beginning. You have no idea who Lamont is and just how he affected my life. You've heard of him but you don't know him. I'll help refresh you on where you've saw him mentioned. Go to your old "Sex & Attention" book and turn to page 1.

"I was abstaining from sex in hopes of being blessed with a husband and giving myself to him. Hilariously, the man I had *loved all my life* dumped me and married some chick with three kids and no high school diploma."

That man. The one I loved all my life. The one who left me and married someone else. Yep. That's Lamont.

I braced myself and I opened his message.

It was a picture of some papers. I read closely. They were divorce papers. His message said.

Lamont Ivy

I did it Book.

I DID IT?

I looked around to be sure Kich wasn't near. I immediately felt guilty. Everyone thought Zay was my biggest weakness but he wasn't… he never was. No one ever would've existed had I been with Lamont. I pushed him to the back of my mind to cope. I didn't know what this meant for my perfect life I had created in my head. I felt like it all was about to come tumbling down. I felt like the mask I had been wearing for years was about to come off and all was going to be revealed. I felt like I was going to have to make the biggest choice of my life.

THE END